THE LADY
WITH THE DOG

and Other Love Stories

THE LADY
WITH THE DOG

and Other Love Stories

DOVER THRIFT EDITIONS

Anton Chekhov

DOVER PUBLICATIONS
GARDEN CITY, NEW YORK

DOVER THRIFT EDITIONS

GENERAL EDITOR: SUSAN L. RATTINER
EDITOR OF THIS VOLUME: JANET B. KOPITO

Bibliographical Note

This Dover edition, first published in 2021, is a new collection of eleven short stories written by Anton Chekhov, reprinted from standard editions. The story translations are by Constance Garnett, except for the following: "About Love" (retranslated by Lydia Razran Stone from Constance Garnett's original translation; "The Beauties" and "After the Theater" (translated by Bob Blaisdell); and "The Darling" (translated by Thomas Seltzer). The story introductions and footnotes, as well as a new introductory Note, have been specially prepared for this edition by Bob Blaisdell.

Library of Congress Cataloging-in-Publication Data

Names: Chekhov, Anton Pavlovich, 1860–1904, author. | Garnett, Constance, 1861–1946, translator. | Blaisdell, Robert, translator. | Stone, Lydia Razran, translator. | Seltzer, Thomas, translator.
Title: The lady with the dog and other love stories / Anton Chekhov ; [translated by Constance Garnett, Bob Blaisdell, Lydia Razran Stone, Thomas Seltzer].
Description: Garden City, New York : Dover Publications, 2021. | Series: Dover thrift editions | Summary: "A master playwright and short story writer, Anton Chekhov is revered for his ability to examine the social forces in his characters' lives. His virtuosity with the written word is on full display in this collection of his best stories that explore the euphoria and despair inherent in the process of falling and being in love. Eleven stories, including 'A Misfortune,' 'Verochka,' 'About Love,' and 'The Lady with the Dog,' offer readers a unique view into one of the most universal human experiences"—Provided by publisher.
Identifiers: LCCN 2021033821 | ISBN 9780486849249 (paperback)
Subjects: LCSH: Chekhov, Anton Pavlovich, 1860–1904—Translations into English. | BISAC: FICTION / Classics | FICTION / General | LCGFT: Romance fiction. | Short stories.
Classification: LCC PG3456.A15 G3 2021 | DDC 891.73/3—dc23
LC record available at https://lccn.loc.gov/2021033821

Manufactured in the United States of America
84924401   2021
www.doverpublications.com

Note

> What she needed was a love that would absorb her whole
> being, her reason, her whole soul, that would give her
> ideas, an object in life.
>
> —"The Darling" (1899)

ANTON PAVLOVICH CHEKHOV, as popular worldwide as any Russian who ever lived, was born in 1860. He was the grandson of a serf who had bought himself and his family out of serfdom. Anton, the third son of his parents' talented six children, was raised in the depressed southern port city of Taganrog, where his abusive father, Pavel, ran a grocery shop. When the shop was mismanaged into bankruptcy, Chekhov's parents and four of Anton's siblings skipped town to Moscow, and left the sixteen-year-old Anton behind to finish high school while working as a tutor. At the age of nineteen Chekhov won a university scholarship from Taganrog's town council and joined the family in Moscow. He immediately became the family's moral and financial backbone and supported his parents and younger siblings while he was in medical school by writing humorous stories, skits, and journalism for newspapers in Moscow and St. Petersburg. At the age of twenty-four, he was a licensed doctor but already infected with the tuberculosis that would kill him at forty-four. He joked that medicine was his lawfully wedded wife and literature his mistress, between which he found freedom as both a doctor and a writer.

The comic tales he wrote under the pseudonym "Antosha Chekhonte" were famous across a wide range of readership. With his own name, writing for prominent magazines, he became the toast of literary Russia. In the bustling years of 1886–87, he wrote more than a hundred short stories, dozens of which are as brilliant and touching as those he wrote at a more measured pace in the years following. Though socially reserved and leery of marriage, he almost invariably remained friends with his former romantic partners, of whom there were several, and he was beloved by friends, editors, fellow writers, and patients. It was only late in life, similar to the hero of "The Lady with the Dog," that he fell truly in love; in 1901 he married the actor Olga Knipper. Debilitated by tuberculosis, Chekhov was supposed to spend the cold parts of the year at the home he bought in Yalta, where he lived with his sister and widowed mother, but he regularly visited Olga in Moscow, where she continued her career, sometimes even acting in her husband's plays. To the end, he denied or minimized to friends and family the diagnosis of his illness and the extent of most of his suffering. In June 1904, Olga accompanied him to a health resort in Germany, where he died the following month.

These eleven stories are "about love"—its psychology and physiology. That is, what does it feel like upstairs and downstairs? What are its symptoms? The eyes of a close observer might notice the signs before the lover does. Chekhov often describes the unconscious feelings of love, and he suggests that love may well feel and *look* like torment. Love's elation is seemingly as agonizing as love's despair. Dmitri Gurov and Anna Sergeyevna, the heroes of "The Lady with the Dog," who are married—but not to each other—could not be more unhappy about their situation . . . *because* they love each other. And so they suffer, despite making of it the best they can: "Anna Sergeyevna and he loved each other like people very close and akin, like husband and wife, like tender friends; it seemed to them that fate itself had meant them for one another, and they could not understand why he had a wife and she a husband; and it was as though they were a pair of birds of passage, caught and forced to live in different cages. They forgave each other for what they were ashamed of in their past, they forgave everything in the present, and felt that this love of theirs had changed them both."

The happiest love stories in this anthology—"After the Theater" and "The Darling"—are comedies, as we smile or laugh at the characters' innocent plights. There is also comedy in the saddest stories because Chekhov couldn't help noticing the differences between what we are supposed to feel and what we do feel, between what a love story should be and what it actually is: absurd, desperate, and as compelling as fate. As we read in "Verochka": "Laughing, crying with tears glistening on her eyelashes, she told him that from the first day of their acquaintance he had struck her by his originality, his intelligence, his kind intelligent eyes, by his work and objects in life; that she loved him passionately, deeply, madly; that when coming into the house from the garden in the summer she saw his cape in the hall or heard his voice in the distance, she felt a cold shudder at her heart, a foreboding of happiness; even his slightest jokes had made her laugh; in every figure in his note-books she saw something extraordinarily wise and grand; his knotted stick seemed to her more beautiful than the trees."

Among the many qualities of these stories, a conspicuous one is the marvelous variety of points of view they take, from the bystanding narrator of "Agafya" to the nonstop dialogue at a fabric store between a spurned shop clerk and a dressmaker ("Polinka") to the awakened memory of boyhood's confusion over the power of physical attraction ("The Beauties") to a teenage girl's longing for romance ("After the Theater") to the storytelling among friends of "About Love," and the subdued but ironical narrator, the one we might as well call Chekhov himself, of the others.

Chekhov tries to leave the moralizing about his stories to his readers. He shows us lovers' dilemmas, and we come to understand with the lovers that there may be no satisfactory resolutions. His refusal to pronounce his judgment of the very characters that he has laid bare to us demonstrates one of his artistic principles: "The artist is not meant to be a judge of his characters and what they say; his only job is to be an impartial witness. . . . Drawing conclusions is up to the jury, that is, the readers."[1] The authors of the best book in English on Chekhov insist, "The very concepts of 'adultery,' 'adultress,' 'the fallen woman,' so very important in Russian literature of the Victorian age, simply do not exist as far as Chekhov is concerned. The fact that a man and a woman not married to each other may sleep together has no moral or immoral dimensions or value in his stories and plays."[2] Chekhov knows that through understanding these "adulterers," we might sympathize with and even—dare we admit it?—envy them, tormented by their passions though they may be.

---

[1] *Anton Chekhov's Life and Thought*, trans. Michael Henry Heim and Simon Karlinsky, commentary by Simon Karlinsky (Berkeley: University of California Press, 1975), 104. [Letter to Alexei Suvorin, 30 May 1888.]

[2] *Anton Chekhov's Life and Thought*, 17.

The translations are by Constance Garnett (1861–1946), unless noted. Her dozen volumes of translations of Chekhov's stories in the 1910s and early 1920s helped make him what he is today, the most popular and famous short story author in the English-speaking world. A hundred years on, her translations remain light, fresh, lively. The only thing lacking in her and everyone else's translations (including mine) is the murmuring, merry buzz communicated through Chekhov's Russian-language voice.

I include the Russian title of each story and the year of its first publication with occasional footnotes about Chekhov's later published revisions. An artist of efficiency and grace, he packed into short stories what others can barely gather into novels. The translations of the texts come from the final edition of his works, a project he undertook in 1899–1901. As he prepared stories for book publication and then for his collected works, his revisions were almost only deletions.

However much I admire Garnett's translations, I have allowed myself to retransliterate names that she extended or modified for what she believed was easier pronunciation (e.g., her *Verotchka* to Verochka and *Dmitritch* to Dmitrich)[3]. I have changed British spellings to American ones ("honour" to honor, etc.), and once every blue moon, I have revised an English word that would cause a twenty-first-century reader more confusion than enlightenment: "groyne" to *pier*, "not worth a farthing" to *not worth a nickel*, "copse" to *grove*, and "make love" to *woo*.

I thank my friends Caroline Allen, Matthew Flamm, Max Schott, and John Wilson for their suggestions of stories for this selection, and I am grateful to Fiona Hallowell at Dover Publications for her encouragement of and support for this project.

BOB BLAISDELL

---

[3] The fondness of Russians for nicknames can flummox English readers: Sofya, for example, can be transformed into, among other renderings, Sonia, Sonichka, or Sofochka.

Contents

THE LADY
WITH THE DOG
and Other Love Stories

AGAFYA

(*Агафья*, 1886)

"Agafya" could just as well be titled "Savka," after the hapless protagonist whose sex appeal to the local women neither Savka nor the narrator fully understands: "He behaved carelessly, condescendingly with them, and even stooped to scornful laughter of their feelings for himself. God knows, perhaps this careless, contemptuous manner was one of the causes of his irresistible attraction for the village Dulcineas. He was handsome and well-built; in his eyes there was always a soft friendliness, even when he was looking at the women he so despised, but the fascination was not to be explained by merely external qualities. Apart from his happy exterior and original manner, one must suppose that the touching position of Savka as an acknowledged failure and an unhappy exile from his own hut to the kitchen gardens also had an influence upon the women." In its original publication, the narrator muses about Agafya, the young married woman who seeks out Savka one night: "What restless force was driving this moth to the flame?"

The narrator's "district of S——" resembles the district a couple of dozen miles from Moscow, near present-day Istra, containing Babkino, where Chekhov rented a summer place for himself, his parents and siblings, and his friends. Though Chekhov was a conscientious doctor and in the midst of the most productive literary period of his life, he insisted, as does the story's narrator, that he was lazy and most enjoyed doing nothing at all.

DURING MY STAY in the district of S—— I often used to go to see the watchman Savva Stukach, or simply Savka, in the kitchen

1

gardens of Dubovo. These kitchen gardens were my favorite resort for so-called "mixed" fishing, when one goes out without knowing what day or hour one may return, taking with one every sort of fishing tackle as well as a store of provisions. To tell the truth, it was not so much the fishing that attracted me as the peaceful stroll, the meals at no set time, the talk with Savka, and being for so long face to face with the calm summer nights. Savka was a young man of five-and-twenty, well grown and handsome, and as strong as a flint. He had the reputation of being a sensible and reasonable fellow. He could read and write, and very rarely drank, but as a workman this strong and healthy young man was not worth a nickel. A sluggish, overpowering sloth was mingled with the strength in his muscles, which were strong as cords. Like everyone else in his village, he lived in his own hut, and had his share of land, but neither tilled it nor sowed it, and did not work at any sort of trade. His old mother begged alms at people's windows and he himself lived like a bird of the air; he did not know in the morning what he would eat at midday. It was not that he was lacking in will, or energy, or feeling for his mother; it was simply that he felt no inclination for work and did not recognize the advantage of it. His whole figure suggested unruffled serenity, an innate, almost artistic passion for living carelessly, never with his sleeves tucked up. When Savka's young, healthy body had a physical craving for muscular work, the young man abandoned himself completely for a brief interval to some free but nonsensical pursuit, such as sharpening skates not wanted for any special purpose, or racing about after the peasant women. His favorite attitude was one of concentrated immobility. He was capable of standing for hours at a stretch in the same place with his eyes fixed on the same spot without stirring. He never moved except on impulse, and then only when an occasion presented itself for some rapid and abrupt action: catching a running dog by the tail, pulling off a woman's kerchief, or jumping over a big hole. It need hardly be said that with such parsimony of movement Savka was as poor as a mouse and lived worse than any homeless outcast. As time went on, I suppose he accumulated arrears of taxes and, young and sturdy as he was, he was sent by the commune to do an old man's job—to be watchman and scarecrow in the kitchen gardens. However much they laughed at him for his premature senility he did not object to it. This position, quiet and convenient for motionless contemplation, exactly fitted his temperament.

It happened I was with this Savka one fine May evening. I remember I was lying on a torn and dirty sackcloth cover close to the shanty from which came a heavy, fragrant scent of hay. Clasping my hands under my head I looked before me. At my feet was lying a wooden fork. Behind it Savka's dog Kutka stood out like a black patch, and not a dozen feet from Kutka the ground ended abruptly in the steep bank of the little river. Lying down I could not see the river; I could only see the tops of the young willows growing thickly on the nearer bank, and the twisting, as it were gnawed away, edges of the opposite bank. At a distance beyond the bank on the dark hillside the huts of the village in which Savka lived lay huddling together like frightened young partridges. Beyond the hill the afterglow of sunset still lingered in the sky. One pale crimson streak was all that was left, and even that began to be covered by little clouds as a fire with ash.

A grove with alder-trees, softly whispering, and from time to time shuddering in the fitful breeze, lay, a dark blur, on the right of the kitchen gardens; on the left stretched the immense plain. In the distance, where the eye could not distinguish between the sky and the plain, there was a bright gleam of light. A little way off from me sat Savka. With his legs tucked under him like a Turk and his head hanging, he looked pensively at Kutka. Our hooks with live bait on them had long been in the river, and we had nothing left to do but to abandon ourselves to repose, which Savka, who was never exhausted and always rested, loved so much. The glow had not yet quite died away, but the summer night was already enfolding nature in its caressing, soothing embrace.

Everything was sinking into its first deep sleep except some night bird unfamiliar to me, which indolently uttered a long, protracted cry in several distinct notes like the phrase, "Have you seen Ni-ki-ta?" and immediately answered itself, "Seen him, seen him, seen him!"

"Why is it the nightingales aren't singing tonight?" I asked Savka.

He turned slowly towards me. His features were large, but his face was open, soft, and expressive as a woman's. Then he gazed with his mild, dreamy eyes at the grove, at the willows, slowly pulled a whistle out of his pocket, put it in his mouth, and whistled the note of a hen-nightingale. And at once, as though in answer to his call, a landrail called on the opposite bank.

"There's a nightingale for you . . ." laughed Savka. "Drag–drag! drag–drag! just like pulling at a hook, and yet I bet he thinks he is singing, too."

"I like that bird," I said. "Do you know, when the birds are migrating the landrail does not fly, but runs along the ground? It only flies over the rivers and the sea, but all the rest it does on foot."

"Upon my word, the dog . . ." muttered Savka, looking with respect in the direction of the calling landrail.

Knowing how fond Savka was of listening, I told him all I had learned about the landrail from sportsman's books. From the landrail I passed imperceptibly to the migration of the birds. Savka listened attentively, looking at me without blinking, and smiling all the while with pleasure.

"And which country is most the bird's home? Ours or those foreign parts?" he asked.

"Ours, of course. The bird itself is hatched here, and it hatches out its little ones here in its native country, and they only fly off there to escape being frozen."

"It's interesting," said Savka. "Whatever one talks about it is always interesting. Take a bird now, or a man . . . or take this little stone; there's something to learn about all of them . . . Ah, sir, if I had known you were coming I wouldn't have told a woman to come here this evening . . . She asked to come today."

"Oh, please don't let me be in your way," I said. "I can lie down in the wood . . ."

"What next! She wouldn't have died if she hadn't come till tomorrow . . . If only she would sit quiet and listen, but she always wants to be slobbering . . . You can't have a good talk when she's here."

"Are you expecting Darya?" I asked, after a pause.

"No . . . a new one has asked to come this evening . . . Agafya, the signalman's wife."

Savka said this in his usual passionless, somewhat hollow voice, as though he were talking of tobacco or porridge, while I started with surprise. I knew Agafya . . . She was quite a young peasant woman of nineteen or twenty, who had been married not more than a year before to a railway signalman, a fine young fellow. She lived in the village, and her husband came home there from the line every night.

"Your goings on with the women will lead to trouble, my boy," said I.

"Well, may be . . ."

And after a moment's thought Savka added:

"I've said so to the women; they won't heed me . . . They don't trouble about it, the silly things!"

Silence followed . . . Meanwhile the darkness was growing thicker and thicker, and objects began to lose their contours. The streak behind the hill had completely died away, and the stars were growing brighter and more luminous . . . The mournfully monotonous chirping of the grasshoppers, the call of the landrail, and the cry of the quail did not destroy the stillness of the night, but, on the contrary, gave it an added monotony. It seemed as though the soft sounds that enchanted the ear came, not from birds or insects, but from the stars looking down upon us from the sky . . .

Savka was the first to break the silence. He slowly turned his eyes from black Kutka and said:

"I see you are bored, sir. Let's have supper."

And without waiting for my consent he crept on his stomach into the shanty, rummaged about there, making the whole edifice tremble like a leaf; then he crawled back and set before me my vodka and an earthenware bowl; in the bowl there were baked eggs, lard scones made of rye, pieces of black bread, and something else . . . We had a drink from a little crooked glass that wouldn't stand, and then we fell upon the food . . . Coarse gray salt, dirty, greasy cakes, eggs tough as India-rubber, but how nice it all was!

"You live all alone, but what lots of good things you have," I said, pointing to the bowl. "Where do you get them from?"

"The women bring them," mumbled Savka.

"What do they bring them to you for?"

"Oh . . . from pity."

Not only Savka's menu, but his clothing, too, bore traces of feminine "pity." Thus I noticed that he had on, that evening, a new woven belt and a crimson ribbon on which a copper cross hung round his dirty neck. I knew of the weakness of the fair sex for Savka, and I knew that he did not like talking about it, and so I did not carry my inquiries any further. Besides there was not time to talk . . . Kutka, who had been fidgeting about near us and patiently waiting for scraps, suddenly pricked up his ears and growled. We heard in the distance repeated splashing of water.

"Someone is coming by the ford," said Savka.

Three minutes later Kutka growled again and made a sound like a cough.

"Shsh!" his master shouted at him.

In the darkness there was a muffled thud of timid footsteps, and the silhouette of a woman appeared out of the grove. I recognized her, although it was dark—it was Agafya. She came up to us diffidently and stopped, breathing hard. She was breathless, probably not so much from walking as from fear and the unpleasant sensation everyone experiences in wading across a river at night. Seeing near the shanty not one but two persons, she uttered a faint cry and fell back a step.

"Ah . . . that is you!" said Savka, stuffing a scone into his mouth.

"Ye-es . . . I," she muttered, dropping on the ground a bundle of some sort and looking sideways at me. "Yakov sent his greetings to you and told me to give you . . . something here . . ."

"Come, why tell stories? Yakov!" laughed Savka. "There is no need for lying; the gentleman knows why you have come! Sit down; you shall have supper with us."

Agafya looked sideways at me and sat down irresolutely.

"I thought you weren't coming this evening," Savka said, after a prolonged silence. "Why sit like that? Eat! Or shall I give you a drop of vodka?"

"What an idea!" laughed Agafya; "do you think you have got hold of a drunkard? . . ."

"Oh, drink it up . . . Your heart will feel warmer . . . There!"

Savka gave Agafya the crooked glass. She slowly drank the vodka, ate nothing with it, but drew a deep breath when she had finished.

"You've brought something," said Savka, untying the bundle and throwing a condescending, jesting shade into his voice. "Women can never come without bringing something. Ah, pie and potatoes . . . They live well," he sighed, turning to me. "They are the only ones in the whole village who have got potatoes left from the winter!"

In the darkness I did not see Agafya's face, but from the movement of her shoulders and head it seemed to me that she could not take her eyes off Savka's face. To avoid being the third person at this tryst, I decided to go for a walk and got up. But at that moment a nightingale in the wood suddenly uttered two low contralto notes. Half a minute later it gave a tiny high trill and then, having thus tried its voice, began singing. Savka jumped up and listened.

"It's the same one as yesterday," he said. "Wait a minute."

And, getting up, he went noiselessly to the wood.

"Why, what do you want with it?" I shouted out after him, "Stop!"

Savka shook his hand as much as to say, "Don't shout," and vanished into the darkness. Savka was an excellent sportsman and fisherman when he liked, but his talents in this direction were as completely thrown away as his strength. He was too slothful to do things in the routine way, and vented his passion for sport in useless tricks. For instance, he would catch nightingales only with his hands, would shoot pike with a fowling piece, he would spend whole hours by the river trying to catch little fish with a big hook.

Left alone with me, Agafya coughed and passed her hand several times over her forehead . . . She began to feel a little drunk from the vodka.

"How are you getting on, Agasha?"[1] I asked her, after a long silence, when it began to be awkward to remain mute any longer.

"Very well, thank God . . . Don't tell anyone, sir, will you?" she added suddenly in a whisper.

"That's all right," I reassured her. "But how reckless you are, Agasha! . . . What if Yakov finds out?"

"He won't find out."

But what if he does?"

"No . . . I shall be at home before he is. He is on the line now, and he will come back when the mail train brings him, and from here I can hear when the train's coming . . ."

Agafya once more passed her hand over her forehead and looked away in the direction in which Savka had vanished. The nightingale was singing. Some night bird flew low down close to the ground and, noticing us, was startled, fluttered its wings, and flew across to the other side of the river.

Soon the nightingale was silent, but Savka did not come back. Agafya got up, took a few steps uneasily, and sat down again.

"What is he doing?" she could not refrain from saying. "The train's not coming in tomorrow! I shall have to go right away."

"Savka," I shouted. "Savka."

I was not answered even by an echo. Agafya moved uneasily and sat down again.

---

[1] Agafya is occasionally familiarly referred to as "Agasha" by Savka and the unnamed narrator.

"It's time I was going," she said in an agitated voice. "The train will be here right away! I know when the trains come in."

The poor woman was not mistaken. Before a quarter of an hour had passed a sound was heard in the distance.

Agafya kept her eyes fixed on the grove for a long time and moved her hands impatiently.

"Why, where can he be?" she said, laughing nervously. "Where has the devil carried him? I am going! I really must be going."

Meanwhile the noise was growing more and more distinct. By now one could distinguish the rumble of the wheels from the heavy gasps of the engine. Then we heard the whistle, the train crossed the bridge with a hollow rumble . . . another minute and all was still.

"I'll wait one minute more," said Agafya, sitting down resolutely. "So be it, I'll wait."

At last Savka appeared in the darkness. He walked noiselessly on the crumbling earth of the kitchen gardens and hummed something softly to himself.

"Here's a bit of luck; what do you say to that now?" he said gaily. "As soon as I got up to the bush and began taking aim with my hand it left off singing! Ah, the bald dog! I waited and waited to see when it would begin again, but I had to give it up."

Savka flopped clumsily down to the ground beside Agafya and, to keep his balance, clutched at her waist with both hands.

"Why do you look cross, as though your aunt were your mother?" he asked.

With all his soft-heartedness and good-nature, Savka despised women. He behaved carelessly, condescendingly with them, and even stooped to scornful laughter of their feelings for himself. God knows, perhaps this careless, contemptuous manner was one of the causes of his irresistible attraction for the village Dulcineas. He was handsome and well-built; in his eyes there was always a soft friendliness, even when he was looking at the women he so despised, but the fascination was not to be explained by merely external qualities. Apart from his happy exterior and original manner, one must suppose that the touching position of Savka as an acknowledged failure and an unhappy exile from his own hut to the kitchen gardens also had an influence upon the women.

"Tell the gentleman what you have come here for!" Savka went on, still holding Agafya by the waist. "Come, tell him, you good married woman! Ho-ho! Shall we have another drop of vodka, friend Agasha?"

I got up and, threading my way between the ridges, I walked the length of the kitchen garden. The dark beds looked like flattened-out graves. They smelt of dug earth and the tender dampness of plants beginning to be covered with dew . . . A red light was still gleaming on the left. It winked genially and seemed to smile.

I heard a happy laugh. It was Agafya laughing.

"And the train?" I thought. "The train has come in long ago."

Waiting a little longer, I went back to the shanty. Savka was sitting motionless, his legs crossed like a Turk, and was softly, scarcely audibly humming a song consisting of words of one syllable, something like: "Out on you, fie on you . . . I and you." Agafya, intoxicated by the vodka, by Savka's scornful caresses, and by the stifling warmth of the night, was lying on the earth beside him, pressing her face convulsively to his knees. She was so carried away by her feelings that she did not even notice my arrival.

"Agasha, the train has been in a long time," I said.

"It's time—it's time you were gone," Savka, tossing his head, took up my thought. "What are you sprawling here for? You shameless hussy!"

Agafya started, took her head from his knees, glanced at me, and sank down beside him again.

"You ought to have gone long ago," I said.

Agafya turned round and got up on one knee . . . She was unhappy . . . For half a minute her whole figure, as far as I could distinguish it through the darkness, expressed conflict and hesitation. There was an instant when, seeming to come to herself, she drew herself up to get upon her feet, but then some invincible and implacable force seemed to push her whole body, and she sank down beside Savka again.

"Bother him!" she said, with a wild, guttural laugh, and reckless determination, impotence, and pain could be heard in that laugh.

I strolled quietly away to the grove, and from there down to the river, where our fishing lines were set. The river slept. Some soft, fluffy-petalled flower on a tall stalk touched my cheek tenderly like a child who wants to let one know it's awake. To pass the time I felt for one of the lines and pulled at it. It yielded easily and hung limply—nothing had been caught . . . The further bank and the village could not be seen. A light gleamed in one hut, but soon went out. I felt my way along the bank, found a hollow place which I had noticed in the daylight, and sat down in it as in an arm-chair. I sat there a long time . . . I saw the stars begin to grow misty and lose their brightness; a cool breath passed over the earth like a faint sigh and touched the leaves of the slumbering osiers. . . .

"A-ga-fya!" a hollow voice called from the village. "Agafya!"

It was the husband, who had returned home, and in alarm was looking for his wife in the village. At that moment there came the sound of unrestrained laughter: the wife, forgetful of everything, sought in her intoxication to make up by a few hours of happiness for the misery awaiting her next day.

I dropped asleep.

When I woke up Savka was sitting beside me and lightly shaking my shoulder. The river, the grove, both banks, green and washed, trees and fields—all were bathed in bright morning light. Through the slim trunks of the trees the rays of the newly risen sun beat upon my back.

"So that's how you catch fish?" laughed Savka. "Get up!"

I got up, gave a luxurious stretch, and began greedily drinking in the damp and fragrant air.

"Has Agasha gone?" I asked.

"There she is," said Savka, pointing in the direction of the ford.

I glanced and saw Agafya. Disheveled, with her kerchief dropping off her head, she was crossing the river, holding up her skirt. Her legs were scarcely moving . . .

"The cat knows whose meat it has eaten," muttered Savka, screwing up his eyes as he looked at her. "She goes with her tail hanging down . . . They are sly as cats, these women, and timid as hares . . . She didn't go, silly thing, in the evening when we told her to! Now she will catch it, and they'll flog me again at the peasant court . . . all on account of the women . . ."

Agafya stepped upon the bank and went across the fields to the village. At first she walked fairly boldly, but soon terror and excitement got the upper hand; she turned round fearfully, stopped and took breath.

"Yes, you are frightened!" Savka laughed mournfully, looking at the bright green streak left by Agafya in the dewy grass. "She doesn't want to go! Her husband's been standing waiting for her for a good hour . . . Did you see him?"

Savka said the last words with a smile, but they sent a chill to my heart. In the village, near the furthest hut, Yakov was standing in the road, gazing fixedly at his returning wife. He stood without stirring, and was as motionless as a post. What was he thinking as he looked at her? What words was he preparing to greet her with?

Agafya stood still a little while, looked round once more as though expecting help from us, and went on. I have never seen anyone, drunk or sober, move as she did. Agafya seemed to be shriveled up by her husband's eyes. At one time she moved in zigzags, then she moved her feet up and down without going forward, bending her knees and stretching out her hands, then she staggered back. When she had gone another hundred paces she looked round once more and sat down.

"You ought at least to hide behind a bush . . ." I said to Savka. "If the husband sees you . . ."

"He knows, anyway, who it is Agafya has come from . . . The women don't go to the kitchen garden at night for cabbages—we all know that."

I glanced at Savka's face. It was pale and puckered up with a look of fastidious pity such as one sees in the faces of people watching tortured animals.

"What's fun for the cat is tears for the mouse . . ." he muttered.

Agafya suddenly jumped up, shook her head, and with a bold step went towards her husband. She had evidently plucked up her courage and made up her mind.

A MISFORTUNE

(*Несчастье*, 1886)

No matter how "Neschast'e" is translated—unhappiness, bad luck, misfortune—Chekhov wants to remind us of how keenly conscious the feeling of love makes us of our unrealized desires. As the distraught Ivan Mikhalovich Ilyin addresses Sofya Petrovna Lubyantsev, the married object of his love: "There's a limit to everything—to struggles with Nature, too. Tell me, how can one struggle against madness? If you drink wine, how are you to struggle against intoxication? What am I to do if your image has grown into my soul, and day and night stands persistently before my eyes, like that pine there at this moment? Come, tell me, what hard and difficult thing can I do to get free from this abominable, miserable condition, in which all my thoughts, desires, and dreams are no longer my own, but belong to some demon who has taken possession of me? I love you, love you so much that I am completely thrown out of gear; I've given up my work and all who are dear to me; I've forgotten my God! I've never been in love like this in my life."

The story takes place in a dacha community outside St. Petersburg or Moscow. In the late nineteenth century dachas were simple cabins where middle-class city residents could venture by train to spend summer months. The heads of households might come out for the weekend, while their wives and children enjoyed fresh air and recreation.

SOFYA PETROVNA, THE wife of Lubyantsev the notary, a handsome young woman of five-and-twenty, was walking slowly along a track that had been cleared in the wood, with Ilyin, a lawyer who

12

was spending the summer in the neighborhood. It was five o'clock in the evening. Feathery-white masses of cloud stood overhead; patches of bright blue sky peeped out between them. The clouds stood motionless, as though they had caught in the tops of the tall old pine-trees. It was still and sultry.

Farther on, the track was crossed by a low railway embankment on which a sentinel with a gun was for some reason pacing up and down. Just beyond the embankment there was a large white church with six domes and a rusty roof.

"I did not expect to meet you here," said Sofya Petrovna, looking at the ground and prodding at the last year's leaves with the tip of her parasol, "and now I am glad we have met. I want to speak to you seriously and once for all. I beg you, Ivan Mikhalovich, if you really love and respect me, please make an end of this pursuit of me! You follow me about like a shadow, you are continually looking at me not in a nice way, wooing me, writing me strange letters, and . . . and I don't know where it's all going to end! Why, what can come of it?"

Ilyin said nothing. Sofya Petrovna walked on a few steps and continued:

"And this complete transformation in you all came about in the course of two or three weeks, after five years' friendship. I don't know you, Ivan Mikhalovich!"

Sofya Petrovna stole a glance at her companion. Screwing up his eyes, he was looking intently at the fluffy clouds. His face looked angry, ill-humored, and preoccupied, like that of a man in pain forced to listen to nonsense.

"I wonder you don't see it yourself," Madame Lubyantsev went on, shrugging her shoulders. "You ought to realize that it's not a very nice part you are playing. I am married; I love and respect my husband. . . . I have a daughter . . . . Can you think all that means nothing? Besides, as an old friend you know my attitude to family life and my views as to the sanctity of marriage."

Ilyin cleared his throat angrily and heaved a sigh.

"Sanctity of marriage . . ." he muttered. "Oh, Lord!"

"Yes, yes. . . . I love my husband, I respect him; and in any case I value the peace of my home. I would rather let myself be killed than be a cause of unhappiness to Andrey and his daughter. . . . And I beg you, Ivan Mikhalovich, for God's sake, leave me in peace! Let us be as good, true friends as we used to be, and give up these sighs and groans, which really don't suit you. It's settled and over! Not a word more about it. Let us talk of something else."

Sofya Petrovna again stole a glance at Ilyin's face. Ilyin was looking up; he was pale, and was angrily biting his quivering lips. She could not understand why he was angry and why he was indignant, but his pallor touched her.

"Don't be angry; let us be friends," she said affectionately. "Agreed? Here's my hand."

Ilyin took her plump little hand in both of his, squeezed it, and slowly raised it to his lips.

"I am not a schoolboy," he muttered. "I am not in the least tempted by friendship with the woman I love."

"Enough, enough! It's settled and done with. We have reached the seat; let us sit down."

Sofya Petrovna's soul was filled with a sweet sense of relief: the most difficult and delicate thing had been said, the painful question was settled and done with. Now she could breathe freely and look Ilyin straight in the face. She looked at him, and the egoistic feeling of the superiority of the woman over the man who loves her, agreeably flattered her. It pleased her to see this huge, strong man, with his manly, angry face and his big black beard—clever, cultivated, and, people said, talented—sit down obediently beside her and bow his head dejectedly. For two or three minutes they sat without speaking.

"Nothing is settled or done with," began Ilyin. "You repeat copy-book maxims to me. 'I love and respect my husband . . . the sanctity of marriage. . . .' I know all that without your help, and I could tell you more, too. I tell you truthfully and honestly that I consider the way I am behaving as criminal and immoral. What more can one say than that? But what's the good of saying what everybody knows? Instead of feeding nightingales with paltry words, you had much better tell me what I am to do."

"I've told you already—go away."

"As you know perfectly well, I have gone away five times, and every time I turned back on the way. I can show you my through tickets—I've kept them all. I have not will enough to run away from you! I am struggling. I am struggling horribly; but what the devil am I good for if I have no backbone, if I am weak, cowardly! I can't struggle with Nature! Do you understand? I cannot! I run away from here, and she holds on to me and pulls me back. Contemptible, loathsome weakness!"

Ilyin flushed crimson, got up, and walked up and down by the seat.

"I feel as cross as a dog," he muttered, clenching his fists. "I hate and despise myself! My God! like some depraved schoolboy, I am wooing another man's wife, writing idiotic letters, degrading myself . . . ugh!"

Ilyin clutched at his head, groaned, and sat down. "And then your insincerity!" he went on bitterly. "If you do dislike my disgusting behavior, why have you come here? What drew you here? In my letters I only ask you for a direct, definite answer—yes or no; but instead of a direct answer, you contrive every day these 'chance' meetings with me and regale me with copy-book maxims!"

Madame Lubyantsev was frightened and flushed. She suddenly felt the awkwardness which a decent woman feels when she is accidentally discovered undressed.

"You seem to suspect I am playing with you," she muttered. "I have always given you a direct answer, and . . . only today I've begged you . . ."

"Ough! as though one begged in such cases! If you were to say straight out 'Get away,' I should have been gone long ago; but you've never said that. You've never once given me a direct answer. Strange indecision! Yes, indeed; either you are playing with me, or else . . ."

Ilyin leaned his head on his fists without finishing. Sofya Petrovna began going over in her own mind the way she had behaved from beginning to end. She remembered that not only in her actions, but even in her secret thoughts, she had always been opposed to Ilyin's wooing; but yet she felt there was a grain of truth in the lawyer's words. But not knowing exactly what the truth was, she could not find answers to make to Ilyin's complaint, however hard she thought. It was awkward to be silent, and, shrugging her shoulders, she said:

"So I am to blame, it appears."

"I don't blame you for your insincerity," sighed Ilyin. "I did not mean that when I spoke of it. . . . Your insincerity is natural and in the order of things. If people agreed together and suddenly became sincere, everything would go to the devil."

Sofya Petrovna was in no mood for philosophical reflections, but she was glad of a chance to change the conversation, and asked:

"But why?"

"Because only savage women and animals are sincere. Once civilization has introduced a demand for such comforts as, for instance, feminine virtue, sincerity is out of place. . . ."

Ilyin jabbed his stick angrily into the sand. Madame Lubyantsev listened to him and liked his conversation, though a great deal of it she did not understand. What gratified her most was that she, an ordinary woman, was talked to by a talented man on "intellectual" subjects; it afforded her great pleasure, too, to watch the working of his mobile, young face, which was still pale and angry. She failed to understand a great deal that he said, but what was clear to her in his words was the attractive boldness with which the modern man without hesitation or doubt decides great questions and draws conclusive deductions.

She suddenly realized that she was admiring him, and was alarmed.

"Forgive me, but I don't understand," she said hurriedly. "What makes you talk of insincerity? I repeat my request again: be my good, true friend; let me alone! I beg you most earnestly!"

"Very good; I'll try again," sighed Ilyin. "Glad to do my best. . . . Only I doubt whether anything will come of my efforts. Either I shall put a bullet through my brains or take to drink in an idiotic way. I shall come to a bad end! There's a limit to everything—to struggles with Nature, too. Tell me, how can one struggle against madness? If you drink wine, how are you to struggle against intoxication? What am I to do if your image has grown into my soul, and day and night stands persistently before my eyes, like that pine there at this moment? Come, tell me, what hard and difficult thing can I do to get free from this abominable, miserable condition, in which all my thoughts, desires, and dreams are no longer my own, but belong to some demon who has taken possession of me? I love you, love you so much that I am completely thrown out of gear; I've given up my work and all who are dear to me; I've forgotten my God! I've never been in love like this in my life."

Sofya Petrovna, who had not expected such a turn to their conversation, drew away from Ilyin and looked into his face in dismay. Tears came into his eyes, his lips were quivering, and there was an imploring, hungry expression in his face.

"I love you!" he muttered, bringing his eyes near her big, frightened eyes. "You are so beautiful! I am in agony now, but I swear I would sit here all my life, suffering and looking in your eyes. But . . . be silent, I implore you!"

Sofya Petrovna, feeling utterly disconcerted, tried to think as quickly as possible of something to say to stop him. "I'll go away," she decided, but before she had time to make a movement to get up, Ilyin was on his knees before her. . . . He was clasping her knees, gazing into her face and speaking passionately, hotly, eloquently. In her terror and confusion she did not hear his words; for some reason now, at this dangerous moment, while her knees were being agreeably squeezed and felt as though they were in a warm bath, she was trying, with a sort of angry spite, to interpret her own sensations. She was angry that instead of brimming over with protesting virtue, she was entirely overwhelmed with weakness, apathy, and emptiness, like a drunken man utterly reckless; only at the bottom of her soul a remote bit of herself was malignantly taunting her: "Why don't you go? Is this as it should be? Yes?"

Seeking for some explanation, she could not understand how it was she did not pull away the hand to which Ilyin was clinging like a leech, and why, like Ilyin, she hastily glanced to right and to left to see whether anyone was looking. The clouds and the pines stood motionless, looking at them severely, like old ushers seeing mischief, but bribed not to tell the school authorities. The sentry stood like a post on the embankment and seemed to be looking at the seat.

"Let him look," thought Sofya Petrovna.

"But . . . but listen," she said at last, with despair in her voice. "What can come of this? What will be the end of this?"

"I don't know, I don't know," he whispered, waving off the disagreeable questions.

They heard the hoarse, discordant whistle of the train. This cold, irrelevant sound from the everyday world of prose made Sofya Petrovna rouse herself.

"I can't stay . . . it's time I was at home," she said, getting up quickly. "The train is coming in. . . Andrey is coming by it! He will want his dinner."

Sofya Petrovna turned towards the embankment with a burning face. The engine slowly crawled by, then came the carriages. It was not the local train, as she had supposed, but a goods train. The trucks filed by against the background of the white church in a long string like the days of a man's life, and it seemed as though it would never end.

But at last the train passed, and the last carriage with the guard and a light in it had disappeared behind the trees. Sofya Petrovna turned round sharply, and without looking at Ilyin, walked rapidly back along the track. She had regained her self-possession. Crimson with shame, humiliated not by Ilyin—no, but by her own cowardice, by the shamelessness with which she, a chaste and high-principled woman, had allowed a man, not her husband, to hug her knees—she had only one thought now: to get home as quickly as possible to her villa, to her family. The lawyer could hardly keep pace with her. Turning from the clearing into a narrow path, she turned round and glanced at him so quickly that she saw nothing but the sand on his knees, and waved to him to drop behind.

Reaching home, Sofya Petrovna stood in the middle of her room for five minutes without moving, and looked first at the window and then at her writing-table.

"You low creature!" she said, upbraiding herself. "You low creature!"

To spite herself, she recalled in precise detail, keeping nothing back—she recalled that though all this time she had been opposed to Ilyin's wooing her, something had impelled her to seek an interview with him; and what was more, when he was at her feet she had enjoyed it enormously. She recalled it all without sparing herself, and now, breathless with shame, she would have liked to slap herself in the face.

"Poor Andrey!" she said to herself, trying as she thought of her husband to put into her face as tender an expression as she could. "Varya, my poor little girl, doesn't know what a mother she has! Forgive me, my dear ones! I love you so much . . . so much!"

And anxious to prove to herself that she was still a good wife and mother, and that corruption had not yet touched that "sanctity of marriage" of which she had spoken to Ilyin, Sofya Petrovna ran to the kitchen and abused the cook for not having yet laid the table for Andrey Ilyich. She tried to picture her husband's hungry and exhausted appearance, commiserated him aloud, and laid the table for him with her own hands, which she had never done before. Then she found her daughter Varya, picked her up in her arms and hugged her warmly; the child seemed to her cold and heavy, but she was unwilling to acknowledge this to herself, and she began explaining to the child how good, kind, and honorable her papa was.

But when Andrey Ilyich arrived soon afterwards she hardly greeted him. The rush of false feeling had already passed off without proving anything to her, only irritating and exasperating her by its falsity. She was sitting by the window, feeling miserable and cross. It is only by being in trouble that people can understand how far from easy it is to be the master of one's feelings and thoughts. Sofya Petrovna said afterwards that there was a tangle within her which it was as difficult to unravel as to count a flock of sparrows rapidly flying by. From the fact that she was not overjoyed to see her husband, that she did not like his manner at dinner, she concluded all of a sudden that she was beginning to hate her husband.

Andrey Ilyich, listless with hunger and exhaustion, fell upon the sausage while waiting for the soup to be brought in, and ate it greedily, munching noisily and moving his temples.

"My goodness!" thought Sofya Petrovna. "I love and respect him, but . . . why does he munch so repulsively?"

The disorder in her thoughts was no less than the disorder in her feelings. Like all persons inexperienced in combating unpleasant ideas, Madame Lubyantsev did her utmost not to think of her trouble, and the harder she tried the more vividly Ilyin, the sand on his knees, the fluffy clouds, the train, stood out in her imagination.

"And why did I go there this afternoon like a fool?" she thought, tormenting herself. "And am I really so weak that I cannot depend upon myself?"

Fear magnifies danger. By the time Andrey Ilyich was finishing the last course, she had firmly made up her mind to tell her husband everything and to flee from danger!

"I've something serious to say to you, Andrey," she began after dinner while her husband was taking off his coat and boots to lie down for a nap.

"Well?"

"Let us leave this place!"

"H'm! . . . Where shall we go? It's too soon to go back to town."

"No; for a tour or something of that sort."

"For a tour . . ." repeated the notary, stretching. "I dream of that myself, but where are we to get the money, and to whom am I to leave the office?"

And thinking a little he added:

"Of course, you must be bored. Go by yourself if you like."

Sofya Petrovna agreed, but at once reflected that Ilyin would be delighted with the opportunity, and would go with her in the same train, in the same compartment. . . . She thought and looked at her husband, now satisfied but still listless. For some reason her eyes rested on his feet—miniature, almost feminine feet, clad in striped socks; there was a thread standing out at the tip of each sock.

Behind the blind a bumblebee was beating itself against the window-pane and buzzing. Sofya Petrovna looked at the threads on the socks, listened to the bee, and pictured how she would set off . . . vis-a-vis Ilyin would sit, day and night, never taking his eyes off her, wrathful at his own weakness and pale with spiritual agony. He would call himself an immoral schoolboy, would abuse her, tear his hair, but when darkness came on and the passengers were asleep or got out at a station, he would seize the opportunity to kneel before her and embrace her knees as he had at the seat in the wood. . . .

She caught herself indulging in this daydream.

"Listen. I won't go alone," she said. "You must come with me."

"Nonsense, Sofochka!" sighed Lubyantsev. "One must be sensible and not want the impossible."

"You will come when you know all about it," thought Sofya Petrovna.

Making up her mind to go at all costs, she felt that she was out of danger. Little by little her ideas grew clearer; her spirits rose and she allowed herself to think about it all, feeling that however much she thought, however much she dreamed, she would go away. While her husband was asleep, the evening gradually came on. She sat in the drawing-room and played the piano. The greater liveliness out of doors, the sound of music, but above all the thought that she was a sensible person, that she had surmounted her difficulties, completely restored her spirits. Other women, her appeased conscience told her, would probably have been carried off their feet in her position, and would have lost their balance, while she had almost died of shame, had been miserable, and was now running out of the danger which perhaps did not exist! She was so touched by her own virtue and determination that she even looked at herself two or three times in the looking-glass.

When it got dark, visitors arrived. The men sat down in the dining-room to play cards; the ladies remained in the drawing-room and the verandah. The last to arrive was Ilyin. He was gloomy, morose, and looked ill. He sat down in the corner of the sofa and did not move the whole evening. Usually good-humored and talkative, this time he remained silent, frowned, and rubbed his eyebrows. When he had to answer some question, he gave a forced smile with his upper lip only, and answered jerkily and irritably.

Four or five times he made some jest, but his jests sounded harsh and cutting. It seemed to Sofya Petrovna that he was on the verge of hysterics. Only now, sitting at the piano, she recognized fully for the first time that this unhappy man was in deadly earnest, that his soul was sick, and that he could find no rest. For her sake he was wasting the best days of his youth and his career, spending the last of his money on a dacha, abandoning his mother and sisters, and, worst of all, wearing himself out in an agonizing struggle with himself. From mere common humanity he ought to be treated seriously.

She recognized all this clearly till it made her heart ache, and if at that moment she had gone up to him and said to him, "No," there would have been a force in her voice hard to disobey. But she did not go up to him and did not speak—indeed, never thought of doing so. The pettiness and egoism of youth had never been more patent in her than that evening. She realized that Ilyin was unhappy, and that he was sitting on the sofa as though he were on hot coals; she felt sorry for him, but at the same time the presence of a man who loved her to distraction, filled her soul with triumph and a sense of her own power. She felt her youth, her beauty, and her unassailable virtue, and, since she had decided to go away, gave herself full license for that evening. She flirted, laughed incessantly, sang with peculiar feeling and gusto. Everything delighted and amused her. She was amused at the memory of what had happened at the seat in the wood, of the sentinel who had looked on. She was amused by her guests, by Ilyin's cutting jests, by the pin in his cravat, which she had never noticed before. There was a red snake with diamond eyes on the pin; this snake struck her as so amusing that she could have kissed it on the spot.

Sofya Petrovna sang nervously, with defiant recklessness as though half intoxicated, and she chose sad, mournful songs which dealt with wasted hopes, the past, old age, as though in mockery of another's grief. " 'And old age comes nearer and nearer' . . ." she sang. And what was old age to her?

"It seems as though there is something going wrong with me," she thought from time to time through her laughter and singing.

The party broke up at twelve o'clock. Ilyin was the last to leave. Sofya Petrovna was still reckless enough to accompany him to the bottom step of the verandah. She wanted to tell him that she was going away with her husband, and to watch the effect this news would produce on him.

The moon was hidden behind the clouds, but it was light enough for Sofya Petrovna to see how the wind played with the skirts of his overcoat and with the awning of the verandah. She could see, too, how white Ilyin was, and how he twisted his upper lip in the effort to smile.

"Sonia, Sonichka . . . my darling woman!" he muttered, preventing her from speaking. "My dear! my sweet!"

In a rush of tenderness, with tears in his voice, he showered caressing words upon her, that grew tenderer and tenderer, and even called her "ty,"[1] as though she were his wife or mistress. Quite unexpectedly he put one arm round her waist and with the other hand took hold of her elbow.

"My precious! my delight!" he whispered, kissing the nape of her neck; "be sincere; come to me at once!"

She slipped out of his arms and raised her head to give vent to her indignation and anger, but the indignation did not come off, and all her vaunted virtue and chastity was only sufficient to enable her to utter the phrase used by all ordinary women on such occasions:

"You must be mad."

"Come, let us go," Ilyin continued. "I felt just now, as well as at the seat in the wood, that you are as helpless as I am, Sonia. . . . You are in the same plight! You love me and are fruitlessly trying to appease your conscience. . . ."

Seeing that she was moving away, he caught her by her lace cuff and said rapidly:

"If not today, then tomorrow you will have to give in! Why, then, this waste of time? My precious, darling Sonia, the sentence is passed; why put off the execution? Why deceive yourself?"

Sofya Petrovna tore herself from him and darted in at the door. Returning to the drawing-room, she mechanically shut the piano, looked for a long time at the music-stand, and sat down. She could not stand up nor think. All that was left of her excitement and recklessness was a fearful weakness, apathy, and dreariness. Her conscience whispered to her that she had behaved badly, foolishly, that evening, like some madcap girl—that she had just been embraced on the verandah, and still had an uneasy feeling in her waist and her elbow. There was not a soul in the drawing-room; there was only one candle burning. Madame Lubyantsev sat on the

---

[1] Ты, the Russian informal "you," analogous to the Spanish *tú* and French *tu*.

round stool before the piano, motionless, as though expecting something. And as though taking advantage of the darkness and her extreme lassitude, an oppressive, overpowering desire began to assail her. Like a boa-constrictor it gripped her limbs and her soul, and grew stronger every second, and no longer menaced her as it had done, but stood clear before her in all its nakedness.

She sat for half an hour without stirring, not restraining herself from thinking of Ilyin, then she got up listlessly and dragged herself to her bedroom. Andrey Ilyich was already in bed. She sat down by the open window and gave herself up to desire. There was no "tangle" now in her head; all her thoughts and feelings were bent with one accord upon a single aim. She tried to struggle against it, but instantly gave it up. . . . She understood now how strong and relentless was the foe. Strength and fortitude were needed to combat him, and her birth, her education, and her life had given her nothing to fall back upon.

"Immoral wretch! Low creature!" she nagged at herself for her weakness. "So that's what you're like!"

Her outraged sense of propriety was moved to such indignation by this weakness that she lavished upon herself every term of abuse she knew, and told herself many offensive and humiliating truths. So, for instance, she told herself that she never had been moral, that she had not come to grief before simply because she had had no opportunity, that her inward conflict during that day had all been a farce. . . .

"And even if I have struggled," she thought, "what sort of struggle was it? Even the woman who sells herself struggles before she brings herself to it, and yet she sells herself. A fine struggle! Like milk, I've turned in a day! In one day!"

She convicted herself of being tempted, not by feeling, not by Ilyin personally, but by sensations which awaited her . . . an idle lady, having her fling in the summer holidays, like so many!

" 'Like an unfledged bird when the mother has been slain,' " sang a husky tenor outside the window.

"If I am to go, it's time," thought Sofya Petrovna. Her heart suddenly began beating violently.

"Andrey!" she almost shrieked. "Listen! We . . . we are going? Yes?"

"Yes, I've told you already: you go alone."

"But listen," she began. "If you don't go with me, you are in danger of losing me. I believe I am . . . in love already."

"With whom?" asked Andrey Ilyich.

"It can't make any difference to you who it is!" cried Sofya Petrovna.

Andrey Ilyich sat up with his feet out of bed and looked wonderingly at his wife's dark figure.

"It's a fancy!" he yawned.

He did not believe her, but yet he was frightened. After thinking a little and asking his wife several unimportant questions, he delivered himself of his opinions on the family, on infidelity . . . spoke listlessly for about ten minutes and got into bed again. His moralizing produced no effect. There are a great many opinions in the world, and a good half of them are held by people who have never been in trouble!

In spite of the late hour, summer visitors were still walking outside. Sofya Petrovna put on a light cape, stood a little, thought a little. . . . She still had resolution enough to say to her sleeping husband:

"Are you asleep? I am going for a walk. . . . Will you come with me?"

That was her last hope. Receiving no answer, she went out. . . . It was fresh and windy. She was conscious neither of the wind nor the darkness, but went on and on. . . . An overmastering force drove her on, and it seemed as though, if she had stopped, it would have pushed her in the back.

"Immoral creature!" she muttered mechanically. "Low wretch!"

She was breathless, hot with shame, did not feel her legs under her, but what drove her on was stronger than shame, reason, or fear.

ON THE ROAD

(*На Пути*, 1886)

In the midst of a year in which he published more than a hundred pieces, Chekhov almost never had a letup in his writing schedule. While carrying on his medical duties, he composed one short story a week for one of three publications as well as a skit or two a week for a humor magazine.

In his midtwenties, whenever Chekhov encountered writer's block, he vaulted over it. For the Christmas issue of the most prominent of the journals for which he was writing, however, he was unusually challenged and explained to his editor: "I began the yuletide story ['On the Road'] two weeks ago and haven't at all finished it. An evil spirit has nudged me toward a theme I can't cope with. After two weeks I succeeded in getting acquainted with the theme and the story and now I don't understand what's good and what's bad. Simply a disaster! Tomorrow, I hope, I'll finish it and send it to you. . . . If you take a look at the story you'll understand the effort with which it was written . . . ."[1]

Likharev, the protagonist of "On the Road," is an idealist. His enthusiasms are so attractive that, to his dismay, he has ruined others whom he has infected with his various intellectual passions. The story's play-like setting is an inn, snowbound during a Christmas-season blizzard. As a young, wealthy woman converses with Likharev during her stopover, she becomes smitten:

"Miss Ilovaisky got up slowly, took a step towards Likharev, and fixed her eyes upon his face. From the tears that glittered on his

---

[1] Anton Chekhov, *Polnoe Sobranie Sochineniy i Pisem: Pis'ma, Tom 1* [Collected Works and Letters: Letters, Vol. 1] (Moscow: Nauka, 1974), 281. [Letter to Alexei Suvorin, 21 December 1886]

*eyelashes, from his quivering, passionate voice, from the flush on
his cheeks, it was clear to her that women were not a chance, not
a simple subject of conversation. They were the object of his new
enthusiasm, or, as he said himself, his new faith! For the first time
in her life she saw a man carried away, fervently believing. With
his gesticulations, with his flashing eyes he seemed to her mad,
frantic, but there was a feeling of such beauty in the fire of his eyes,
in his words, in all the movements of his huge body, that without
noticing what she was doing she stood facing him as though rooted
to the spot, and gazed into his face with delight."*

> Upon the breast of a gigantic crag,
> A golden cloudlet rested for one night.
> —Mikhail Lermontov

IN THE ROOM which the tavern keeper, the Cossack Semyon
Chistopluy, called the "travelers' room," that is kept exclusively for
travelers, a tall, broad-shouldered man of forty was sitting at the big
unpainted table. He was asleep with his elbows on the table and his
head leaning on his fist. An end of tallow candle, stuck into an old
pomatum pot, lighted up his light brown beard, his thick, broad
nose, his sunburnt cheeks, and the thick, black eyebrows overhanging
his closed eyes. . . . The nose and the cheeks and the eyebrows, all
the features, each taken separately, were coarse and heavy, like the
furniture and the stove in the "travelers' room," but taken all
together they gave the effect of something harmonious and even
beautiful. Such is the lucky star, as it is called, of the Russian face:
the coarser and harsher its features the softer and more good-
natured it looks. The man was dressed in a gentleman's peacoat,
shabby, but bound with wide new braid, a plush waistcoat, and full
black trousers thrust into big high boots.

On one of the benches, which stood in a continuous row along
the wall, a girl of eight, in a brown dress and long black stockings,
lay asleep on a coat lined with fox. Her face was pale, her hair was
flaxen, her shoulders were narrow, her whole body was thin and
frail, but her nose stood out as thick and ugly a lump as the man's.
She was sound asleep, and unconscious that her semi-circular comb
had fallen off her head and was cutting her cheek.

The "travelers' room" had a festive appearance. The air was full
of the smell of freshly scrubbed floors, there were no rags hanging
as usual on the line that ran diagonally across the room, and a little

lamp was burning in the corner over the table, casting a patch of red light on the ikon of St. George the Victorious. From the ikon stretched on each side of the corner a row of cheap oleographs, which maintained a strict and careful gradation in the transition from the sacred to the profane. In the dim light of the candle end and the red ikon lamp the pictures looked like one continuous stripe, covered with blurs of black. When the tiled stove, trying to sing in unison with the weather, drew in the air with a howl, while the logs, as though waking up, burst into bright flame and hissed angrily, red patches began dancing on the log walls, and over the head of the sleeping man could be seen first the Elder Seraphim, then the Shah Nasir–ed–Din, then a fat, brown baby with goggle eyes, whispering in the ear of a young girl with an extraordinarily blank and indifferent face. . . .

Outside a storm was raging. Something frantic and wrathful, but profoundly unhappy, seemed to be flinging itself about the tavern with the ferocity of a wild beast and trying to break in. Banging at the doors, knocking at the windows and on the roof, scratching at the walls, it alternately threatened and besought, then subsided for a brief interval, and then with a gleeful, treacherous howl burst into the chimney, but the wood flared up, and the fire, like a chained dog, flew wrathfully to meet its foe, a battle began, and after it— sobs, shrieks, howls of wrath. In all of this there was the sound of angry misery and unsatisfied hate, and the mortified impatience of something accustomed to triumph.

Bewitched by this wild, inhuman music the "travelers' room" seemed spellbound for ever, but all at once the door creaked and the potboy, in a new print shirt, came in. Limping on one leg, and blinking his sleepy eyes, he snuffed the candle with his fingers, put some more wood on the fire, and went out. At once from the church, which was three hundred paces from the tavern, the clock struck midnight. The wind played with the chimes as with the snowflakes; chasing the sounds of the clock it whirled them round and round over a vast space, so that some strokes were cut short or drawn out in long, vibrating notes, while others were completely lost in the general uproar. One stroke sounded as distinctly in the room as though it had chimed just under the window. The child, sleeping on the fox–skin, started and raised her head. For a minute she stared blankly at the dark window, at Nasir–ed–Din over whom a crimson glow from the fire flickered at that moment, then she turned her eyes upon the sleeping man.

"Daddy," she said.

But the man did not move. The little girl knitted her brow angrily, lay down, and curled up her legs. Someone in the tavern gave a loud, prolonged yawn. Soon afterwards there was the squeak of the swing door and the sound of indistinct voices. Someone came in, shaking the snow off, and stamping in felt boots which made a muffled thud.

"What is it?" a woman's voice asked listlessly.

"Mademoiselle Ilovaisky has come, . . ." answered a bass voice.

Again there was the squeak of the swing door. Then came the roar of the wind rushing in. Someone, probably the lame boy, ran to the door leading to the "travelers' room," coughed deferentially, and lifted the latch.

"This way, lady, please," said a woman's voice in dulcet tones. "It's clean in here, my beauty. . . ."

The door was opened wide and a peasant with a beard appeared in the doorway, in the long coat of a coachman, plastered all over with snow from head to foot, and carrying a big trunk on his shoulder. He was followed into the room by a feminine figure, scarcely half his height, with no face and no arms, muffled and wrapped up like a bundle and also covered with snow. A damp chill, as from a cellar, seemed to come to the child from the coachman and the bundle, and the fire and the candles flickered.

"What nonsense!" said the bundle angrily. "We could go perfectly well. We have only nine more miles to go, mostly by the forest, and we should not get lost. . . ."

"As for getting lost, we shouldn't, but the horses can't go on, lady!" answered the coachman. "And it is Thy Will, O Lord! As though I had done it on purpose!"

"God knows where you have brought me. . . . Well, be quiet. . . . There are people asleep here, it seems. You can go. . . ."

The coachman put the portmanteau on the floor, and as he did so, a great lump of snow fell off his shoulders. He gave a sniff and went out.

Then the little girl saw two little hands come out from the middle of the bundle, stretch upwards and begin angrily disentangling the network of shawls, kerchiefs, and scarves. First a big shawl fell on the ground, then a hood, then a white knitted kerchief. After freeing her head, the traveler took off her pelisse and at once shrank to half the size. Now she was in a long, gray coat with big buttons and bulging pockets. From one pocket she pulled out a paper parcel, from the other a bunch of big, heavy keys, which she put down so carelessly that the sleeping man started and opened his eyes. For some time he looked blankly round him as though he didn't know where he was, then he shook his head, went to the corner and sat down. . . . The newcomer took off her great coat, which made her shrink to half her size again; she took off her big felt boots, and sat down, too.

By now she no longer resembled a bundle: she was a thin little brunette of twenty, as slim as a snake, with a long white face and curly hair. Her nose was long and sharp, her chin, too, was long and sharp, her eyelashes were long, the corners of her mouth were sharp, and, thanks to this general sharpness, the expression of her face was biting. Swathed in a closely fitting black dress with a mass of lace at her neck and sleeves, with sharp elbows and long pink fingers, she recalled the portraits of medieval English ladies. The grave concentration of her face increased this likeness.

The lady looked round at the room, glanced sideways at the man and the little girl, shrugged her shoulders, and moved to the window. The dark windows were shaking from the damp west wind. Big flakes of snow glistening in their whiteness, lay on the window frame, but at once disappeared, borne away by the wind. The savage music grew louder and louder. . . .

After a long silence the little girl suddenly turned over, and said angrily, emphasizing each word:

"Oh, goodness, goodness, how unhappy I am! Unhappier than anyone!"

The man got up and moved with little steps to the child with a guilty air, which was utterly out of keeping with his huge figure and big beard.

"You are not asleep, dearie?" he said, in an apologetic voice. "What do you want?"

"I don't want anything, my shoulder aches! You are a wicked man, Daddy, and God will punish you! You'll see He will punish you."

"My darling, I know your shoulder aches, but what can I do, dearie?" said the man, in the tone in which men who have been drinking excuse themselves to their stern spouses. "It's the journey has made your shoulder ache, Sasha. Tomorrow we shall get there and rest, and the pain will go away. . . ."

"Tomorrow, tomorrow. . . . Every day you say tomorrow. We shall be going on another twenty days."

"But we shall arrive tomorrow, dearie, on your father's word of honor. I never tell a lie, but if we are detained by the snowstorm it is not my fault."

"I can't bear any more, I can't, I can't!"

Sasha jerked her leg abruptly and filled the room with an unpleasant wailing. Her father made a despairing gesture, and looked hopelessly towards the young lady. The latter shrugged her shoulders, and hesitatingly went up to Sasha.

"Listen, my dear," she said, "it is no use crying. It's really naughty; if your shoulder aches it can't be helped."

"You see, Madam," said the man quickly, as though defending himself, "we have not slept for two nights, and have been traveling in a revolting conveyance. Well, of course, it is natural she should be ill and miserable, . . . and then, you know, we had a drunken driver, our portmanteau has been stolen . . . the snowstorm all the time, but what's the use of crying, Madam? I am exhausted, though, by sleeping in a sitting position, and I feel as though I were drunk. Oh, Sasha, I feel sick as it is, and then you cry!"

The man shook his head, and with a gesture of despair sat down.

"Of course you mustn't cry," said the young lady. "It's only little babies cry. If you are ill, dear, you must undress and go to sleep. . . . Let us take off your things!"

When the child had been undressed and pacified a silence reigned again. The young lady seated herself at the window, and looked round wonderingly at the room of the inn, at the ikon, at the stove. . . . Apparently the room and the little girl with the thick nose, in her short boy's nightgown, and the child's father, all seemed strange to her. This strange man was sitting in a corner; he kept looking about him helplessly, as though he were drunk, and rubbing his face with the palm of his hand. He sat silent, blinking, and judging from his guilty-looking figure it was difficult to imagine that he would soon begin to speak. Yet he was the first to begin. Stroking his knees, he gave a cough, laughed, and said:

"It's a comedy, it really is. . . . I look and I cannot believe my eyes: for what devilry has destiny driven us to this accursed inn? What did she want to show by it? Life sometimes performs such a 'salto mortale,'[2] one can only stare and blink in amazement. Have you come from far, Madam?"

---

[2] "salto mortale": Italian for *somersault*, or more literally, "deadly jump."

"No, not from far," answered the young lady. "I am going from our estate, fifteen miles from here, to our farm, to my father and brother. My name is Ilovaisky, and the farm is called Ilovaiskoe. It's nine miles away. What unpleasant weather!"

"It couldn't be worse."

The lame boy came in and stuck a new candle in the pomatum pot.

"You might bring us the samovar, boy," said the man, addressing him.

"Who drinks tea now?" laughed the boy. "It is a sin to drink tea before mass. . . ."

"Never mind, boy, you won't burn in hell if we do. . . ."

Over the tea the new acquaintances got into conversation.

Miss Ilovaisky learned that her companion was called Grigory Petrovich Likharev, that he was the brother of the Likharev who was Marshal of Nobility in one of the neighboring districts, and he himself had once been a landowner, but had "run through everything in his time." Likharev learned that her name was Marya Mikhailovna, that her father had a huge estate, but that she was the only one to look after it as her father and brother looked at life through their fingers, were irresponsible, and were too fond of borzois.

"My father and brother are all alone at the farm," she told him, brandishing her fingers (she had the habit of moving her fingers before her pointed face as she talked, and after every sentence moistened her lips with her sharp little tongue). "They, I mean men, are an irresponsible lot, and don't stir a finger for themselves. I can fancy there will be no one to give them a meal after the fast! We have no mother, and we have such servants that they can't lay the tablecloth properly when I am away. You can imagine their condition now! They will be left with nothing to break their fast, while I have to stay here all night. How strange it all is."

She shrugged her shoulders, took a sip from her cup, and said:

"There are festivals that have a special fragrance: at Easter, Trinity and Christmas there is a peculiar scent in the air. Even unbelievers are fond of those festivals. My brother, for instance, argues that there is no God, but he is the first to hurry to Matins at Easter."

Likharev raised his eyes to Miss Ilovaisky and laughed.

"They argue that there is no God," she went on, laughing too, "but why is it, tell me, all the celebrated writers, the learned men, clever people generally, in fact, believe towards the end of their life?"

"If a man does not know how to believe when he is young, Madam, he won't believe in his old age if he is ever so much of a writer."

Judging from Likharev's cough he had a bass voice, but, probably from being afraid to speak aloud, or from exaggerated shyness, he spoke in a tenor. After a brief pause he heaved a sigh and said:

"The way I look at it is that faith is a faculty of the spirit. It is just the same as a talent, one must be born with it. So far as I can judge by myself, by the people I have seen in my time, and by all that is done around us, this faculty is present in Russians in its highest degree. Russian life presents us with an uninterrupted succession of convictions and aspirations, and if you care to know, it has not yet the faintest notion of lack of faith or scepticism. If a Russian does not believe in God, it means he believes in something else."

Likharev took a cup of tea from Miss Ilovaisky, drank off half in one gulp, and went on:

"I will tell you about myself. Nature has implanted in my breast an extraordinary faculty for belief. Whisper it not to the night, but half my life I was in the ranks of the Atheists and Nihilists, but there was not one hour in my life in which I ceased to believe. All talents, as a rule, show themselves in early childhood, and so my faculty showed itself when I could still walk upright under the table. My mother liked her children to eat a great deal, and when she gave me food she used to say: 'Eat! Soup is the great thing in life!' I believed, and ate the soup ten times a day, ate like a shark, ate till I was disgusted and stupefied. My nurse used to tell me fairy tales, and I believed in house-spirits, in wood-elves, and in goblins of all kinds. I used sometimes to steal corrosive sublimate from my father, sprinkle it on cakes, and carry them up to the attic that the house-spirits, you see, might eat them and be killed. And when I was taught to read and understand what I read, then there was a fine to-do. I ran away to 'America' and went off to join the brigands, and wanted to go into a monastery, and hired boys to torture me for being a Christian. And note that my faith was always active, never dead. If I was running away to 'America' I was not alone, but seduced someone else, as great a fool as I was, to go with me, and was delighted when I was nearly frozen outside the town gates and when I was thrashed; if I went to join the brigands I always came back with my face battered. A most restless childhood, I assure you! And when they sent me to the high school and pelted me with all sorts of truths—that is, that the earth goes round the sun, or that white light is not white, but is made up of seven colors—my poor little head began to go round! Everything was thrown into a whirl in me: Navin who made the sun stand still, and my mother who in the name of the Prophet Elijah disapproved of lightning conductors, and my father who was indifferent to the truths I had learned. My enlightenment inspired me. I wandered about the house and stables like one possessed, preaching my truths, was horrified by ignorance, glowed with hatred for anyone who saw in white light nothing but white light. . . . But all that's nonsense and childishness. Serious, so to speak, manly enthusiasms began only at the university. You have, no doubt, Madam, taken your degree somewhere?"

"I studied at Novocherkassk at the Don Institute."

"Then you have not been to a university? So you don't know what science means. All the sciences in the world have the same passport, without which they regard themselves as meaningless . . . the striving towards truth! Every one of them, even pharmacology, has for its aim not utility, not the alleviation of life, but truth. It's remarkable! When you set to work to study any science, what strikes you first of all is its beginning. I assure you there is nothing more attractive and grander, nothing is so staggering, nothing takes a man's breath away like the beginning of any science. From the first five or six lectures you are soaring on wings of the brightest hopes, you already seem to yourself to be welcoming truth with open arms. And I gave myself up to science, heart and soul, passionately, as to the woman one loves. I was its slave; I found it the sun of my existence, and asked for no other. I studied day and night without rest, ruined myself over books, wept when before my eyes men exploited science for their own personal ends. But my enthusiasm did not last long. The trouble is that every science has a beginning but not an end, like a recurring decimal. Zoology has discovered 35,000 kinds of insects, chemistry reckons 60 elements. If in time tens of zeroes can be written after these figures, zoology and chemistry will be just as far from their end as now, and all contemporary scientific work consists in increasing these numbers. I saw through this trick when I discovered the thirty-five thousand and first and felt no satisfaction. Well, I had no time to suffer from disillusionment, as I was soon possessed by a new faith. I plunged into Nihilism, with its manifestoes, its 'black divisions,' and all the rest of it. I 'went to the people,' worked in factories, worked as an oiler, as a barge hauler. Afterwards, when wandering over Russia,

I had a taste of Russian life, I turned into a fervent devotee of that life. I loved the Russian people with poignant intensity; I loved their God and believed in Him, and in their language, their creative genius. . . . And so on, and so on. . . . I have been a Slavophile in my time, I used to pester Aksakov with letters, and I was a Ukrainophile, and an archeologist, and a collector of specimens of peasant art. . . . I was enthusiastic over ideas, people, events, places . . . my enthusiasm was endless! Five years ago I was working for the abolition of private property; my last creed was non-resistance to evil."

Sasha gave an abrupt sigh and began moving. Likharev got up and went to her.

"Won't you have some tea, dearie?" he asked tenderly.

"Drink it yourself," the child answered rudely. Likharev was disconcerted, and went back to the table with a guilty step.

"Then you have had a lively time," said Miss Ilovaisky; "you have something to remember."

"Well, yes, it's all very lively when one sits over tea and chatters to a kind listener, but you should ask what that liveliness has cost me! What price have I paid for the variety of my life? You see, Madam, I have not held my convictions like a German doctor of philosophy, I have not lived in solitude, but every conviction I have had has bound my back to the yoke, has torn my body to pieces. Judge, for yourself. I was wealthy like my brothers, but now I am a beggar. In the delirium of my enthusiasm I smashed up my own fortune and my wife's—a heap of other people's money. Now I am forty-two, old age is close upon me, and I am homeless, like a dog that has dropped behind its wagon at night. All my life I have not known what peace meant, my soul has been in continual agitation, distressed even by its hopes . . . I have been wearied out with heavy irregular work, have endured privation, have five times been in prison, have dragged myself across the provinces of Archangel and of Tobolsk . . . it's painful to think of it! I have lived, but in my fever I have not even been conscious of the process of life itself. Would you believe it, I don't remember a single spring, I never noticed how my wife loved me, how my children were born. What more can I tell you? I have been a misfortune to all who have loved me. . . . My mother has worn mourning for me all these fifteen years, while my proud brothers, who have had to wince, to blush, to bow their heads, to waste their money on my account, have come in the end to hate me like poison."

Likharev got up and sat down again.

"If I were simply unhappy I should thank God," he went on without looking at his listener. "My personal unhappiness sinks into the background when I remember how often in my enthusiasms I have been absurd, far from the truth, unjust, cruel, dangerous! How often I have hated and despised those whom I ought to have loved, and vice versa, I have changed a thousand times. One day I believe, fall down and worship, the next I flee like a coward from the gods and friends of yesterday, and swallow in silence the 'scoundrel!' they hurl after me. God alone has seen how often I have wept and bitten my pillow in shame for my enthusiasms. Never once in my life have I intentionally lied or done evil, but my conscience is not clear! I cannot even boast, Madam, that I have no one's life upon my conscience, for my wife died before my eyes, worn out by my reckless activity. Yes, my wife! I tell you they have two ways of treating women nowadays. Some measure women's skulls to prove woman is inferior to man, pick out her defects to mock at her, to look original in her eyes, and to justify their sensuality. Others do their utmost to raise women to their level, that is, force them to learn by heart the 35,000 species, to speak and write the same foolish things as they speak and write themselves."

Likharev's face darkened.

"I tell you that woman has been and always will be the slave of man," he said in a bass voice, striking his fist on the table. "She is the soft, tender wax which a man always molds into anything he likes. . . . My God! for the sake of some trumpery masculine enthusiasm she will cut off her hair, abandon her family, die among strangers! . . . among the ideas for which she has sacrificed herself there is not a single feminine one. . . . An unquestioning, devoted slave! I have not measured skulls, but I say this from hard, bitter experience: the proudest, most independent women, if I have succeeded in communicating to them my enthusiasm, have followed me without criticism, without question, and done anything I chose; I have turned a nun into a Nihilist who, as I heard afterwards, shot a gendarme; my wife never left me for a minute in my wanderings, and like a weathercock changed her faith in step with my changing enthusiasms."

Likharev jumped up and walked up and down the room.

"A noble, sublime slavery!" he said, clasping his hands. "It is just in it that the highest meaning of woman's life lies! Of all the fearful medley of thoughts and impressions accumulated in my brain from

my association with women my memory, like a filter, has retained
no ideas, no clever saying, no philosophy, nothing but that
extraordinary, resignation to fate, that wonderful mercifulness,
forgiveness of everything."

Likharev clenched his fists, stared at a fixed point, and with a sort
of passionate intensity, as though he were savoring each word as he
uttered it, hissed through his clenched teeth:

"That . . . that great-hearted fortitude, faithfulness unto death,
poetry of the heart. . . . The meaning of life lies in just that
unrepining martyrdom, in the tears which would soften a stone, in
the boundless, all-forgiving love which brings light and warmth
into the chaos of life. . . ."

Miss Ilovaisky got up slowly, took a step towards Likharev, and
fixed her eyes upon his face. From the tears that glittered on his
eyelashes, from his quivering, passionate voice, from the flush on
his cheeks, it was clear to her that women were not a chance, not
a simple subject of conversation. They were the object of his new
enthusiasm, or, as he said himself, his new faith! For the first time
in her life she saw a man carried away, fervently believing. With his
gesticulations, with his flashing eyes he seemed to her mad, frantic,
but there was a feeling of such beauty in the fire of his eyes, in his
words, in all the movements of his huge body, that without
noticing what she was doing she stood facing him as though rooted
to the spot, and gazed into his face with delight.

"Take my mother," he said, stretching out his hand to her with
an imploring expression on his face, "I poisoned her existence,
according to her ideas disgraced the name of Likharev, did her as
much harm as the most malignant enemy, and what do you think?
My brothers give her little sums for holy bread and church services,
and outraging her religious feelings, she saves that money and sends
it in secret to her erring Grigory. This trifle alone elevates and
ennobles the soul far more than all the theories, all the clever sayings
and the 35,000 species. I can give you thousands of instances. Take
you, even, for instance! With tempest and darkness outside you are
going to your father and your brother to cheer them with your
affection in the holiday, though very likely they have forgotten and
are not thinking of you. And, wait a bit, and you will love a man
and follow him to the North Pole. You would, wouldn't you?"

"Yes, if I loved him."

"There, you see," cried Likharev delighted, and he even stamped
with his foot. "Oh dear! How glad I am that I have met you! Fate

is kind to me, I am always meeting splendid people. Not a day passes but one makes acquaintance with somebody one would give one's soul for. There are ever so many more good people than bad in this world. Here, see, for instance, how openly and from our hearts we have been talking as though we had known each other a hundred years. Sometimes, I assure you, one restrains oneself for ten years and holds one's tongue, is reserved with one's friends and one's wife, and meets some cadet in a train and babbles one's whole soul out to him. It is the first time I have the honor of seeing you, and yet I have confessed to you as I have never confessed in my life. Why is it?"

Rubbing his hands and smiling good-humoredly Likharev walked up and down the room, and fell to talking about women again. Meanwhile they began ringing for matins.

"Goodness," wailed Sasha. "He won't let me sleep with his talking!"

"Oh, yes!" said Likharev, startled. "I am sorry, darling, sleep, sleep. . . . I have two boys besides her," he whispered. "They are living with their uncle, Madam, but this one can't exist a day without her father. She's wretched, she complains, but she sticks to me like a fly to honey. I have been chattering too much, Madam, and it would do you no harm to sleep. Wouldn't you like me to make up a bed for you?"

Without waiting for permission he shook the wet pelisse, stretched it on a bench, fur side upwards, collected various shawls and scarves, put the overcoat folded up into a roll for a pillow, and all this he did in silence with a look of devout reverence, as though he were not handling a woman's rags, but the fragments of holy vessels. There was something apologetic, embarrassed about his whole figure, as though in the presence of a weak creature he felt ashamed of his height and strength. . . .

When Miss Ilovaisky had lain down, he put out the candle and sat down on a stool by the stove.

"So, Madam," he whispered, lighting a fat cigarette and puffing the smoke into the stove. "Nature has put into the Russian an extraordinary faculty for belief, a searching intelligence, and the gift of speculation, but all that is reduced to ashes by irresponsibility, laziness, and dreamy frivolity. . . . Yes. . . ."

She gazed wonderingly into the darkness, and saw only a spot of red on the ikon and the flicker of the light of the stove on Likharev's face. The darkness, the chime of the bells, the roar of the storm, the lame boy, Sasha with her fretfulness, unhappy Likharev and his sayings—all this was mingled together, and seemed to grow into one huge impression, and God's world seemed to her fantastic, full of marvels and magical forces. All that she had heard was ringing in her ears, and human life presented itself to her as a beautiful poetic fairy-tale without an end.

The immense impression grew and grew, clouded consciousness, and turned into a sweet dream. She was asleep, though she saw the little ikon lamp and a big nose with the light playing on it.

She heard the sound of weeping.

"Daddy, darling," a child's voice was tenderly entreating, "let's go back to uncle! There is a Christmas-tree there! Styopa and Kolya are there!"

"My darling, what can I do?" a man's bass persuaded softly. "Understand me! Come, understand!"

And the man's weeping blended with the child's. This voice of human sorrow, in the midst of the howling of the storm, touched the girl's ear with such sweet human music that she could not bear the delight of it, and wept too. She was conscious afterwards of a big, black shadow coming softly up to her, picking up a shawl that had dropped on to the floor, and carefully wrapping it round her feet.

Miss Ilovaisky was awakened by a strange uproar. She jumped up and looked about her in astonishment. The deep blue dawn was looking in at the window half-covered with snow. In the room there was a gray twilight, through which the stove and the sleeping child and Nasir-ed-Din stood out distinctly. The stove and the lamp were both out. Through the wide-open door she could see the big tavern room with a counter and chairs. A man, with a stupid face and astonished eyes, was standing in the middle of the room in a puddle of melting snow, holding a big red star on a stick. He was surrounded by a group of boys, motionless as statues, and plastered over with snow. The light shone through the red paper of the star, throwing a glow of red on their wet faces. The crowd was shouting in disorder, and from its uproar Miss Ilovaisky could make out only one couplet.

Likharev was standing near the counter, looking feelingly at the singers and tapping his feet in time. Seeing Miss Ilovaisky, he smiled all over his face and came up to her. She smiled too.

"A happy Christmas!" he said. "I saw you slept well."

She looked at him, said nothing, and went on smiling.

After the conversation in the night he seemed to her not tall and broad shouldered, but little, just as the biggest steamer seems to us a little thing when we hear that it has crossed the ocean.

"Well, it is time for me to set off," she said. "I must put on my things. Tell me where you are going now?"

"I? To the station of Klinushki, from there to Sergievo, and from Sergievo, with horses, thirty miles to the coal mines that belong to a horrid man, a general called Shashkovsky. My brothers have got me the post of superintendent there. . . . I am going to be a coal miner."

"Stay, I know those mines. Shashkovsky is my uncle, you know. But . . . what are you going there for?" asked Miss Ilovaisky, looking at Likharev in surprise.

"As superintendent. To superintend the coal mines."

"I don't understand!" she shrugged her shoulders. "You are going to the mines. But you know, it's the bare steppe, a desert, so dreary that you couldn't exist a day there! It's horrible coal, no one will buy it, and my uncle's a maniac, a despot, a bankrupt. . . . You won't get your salary!"

"No matter," said Likharev, unconcernedly, "I am thankful even for coal mines."

She shrugged her shoulders, and walked about the room in agitation.

"I don't understand, I don't understand," she said, moving her fingers before her face. "It's impossible, and . . . and irrational! You must understand that it's . . . it's worse than exile. It is a living tomb! O Heavens!" she said hotly, going up to Likharev and moving her fingers before his smiling face; her upper lip was quivering, and her sharp face turned pale, "Come, picture it, the bare steppe, solitude. There is no one to say a word to there, and you . . . are enthusiastic over women! Coal mines . . . and women!"

Miss Ilovaisky was suddenly ashamed of her heat and, turning away from Likharev, walked to the window.

"No, no, you can't go there," she said, moving her fingers rapidly over the pane.

Not only in her heart, but even in her spine she felt that behind her stood an infinitely unhappy man, lost and outcast, while he, as though he were unaware of his unhappiness, as though he had not shed tears in the night, was looking at her with a kindly smile. Better he should go on weeping! She walked up and down the room several times in agitation, then stopped short in a corner and sank into thought. Likharev was saying something, but she did not hear him. Turning her back on him she took out of her purse a money note, stood for a long time crumpling it in her hand, and looking round at Likharev, blushed and put it in her pocket.

The coachman's voice was heard through the door. With a stern, concentrated face she began putting on her things in silence. Likharev wrapped her up, chatting gaily, but every word he said lay on her heart like a weight. It is not cheering to hear the unhappy or the dying jest.

When the transformation of a live person into a shapeless bundle had been completed, Miss Ilovaisky looked for the last time round the "travelers' room," stood a moment in silence, and slowly walked out. Likharev went to see her off. . . .

Outside, God alone knows why, the winter was raging still. Whole clouds of big soft snowflakes were whirling restlessly over the earth, unable to find a resting-place. The horses, the sledge, the trees, a bull tied to a post, all were white and seemed soft and fluffy.

"Well, God help you," muttered Likharev, tucking her into the sledge. "Don't remember evil against me . . . ."

She was silent. When the sledge started, and had to go round a huge snowdrift, she looked back at Likharev with an expression as though she wanted to say something to him. He ran up to her, but she did not say a word to him, she only looked at him through her long eyelashes with little specks of snow on them.

Whether his finely intuitive soul were really able to read that look, or whether his imagination deceived him, it suddenly began to seem to him that with another touch or two that girl would have forgiven him his failures, his age, his desolate position, and would have followed him without question or reasonings. He stood a long while as though rooted to the spot, gazing at the tracks left by the sledge runners. The snowflakes greedily settled on his hair, his beard, his shoulders. . . . Soon the track of the runners had vanished, and he himself covered with snow, began to look like a white rock, but still his eyes kept seeking something in the clouds of snow.

POLINKA

(*Полинька*, 1887)

As a boy Chekhov had to tend his father's grocery shop after school and serve customers, all while trying to study. As an adult, his sympathies were always with working-class people. We see class consciousness and a broken heart in this story-long dialogue between a fabric-store clerk and a dressmaker: " 'Pretend to be looking at the things,' Nikolai Timofeich whispers, bending down to Polinka with a forced smile. 'Dear me, you do look pale and ill; you are quite changed. He'll throw you over, Pelagea Sergeevna! Or if he does marry you, it won't be for love but from hunger; he'll be tempted by your money. He'll furnish himself a nice home with your dowry, and then be ashamed of you. He'll keep you out of sight of his friends and visitors, because you're uneducated. He'll call you "my dummy of a wife." You wouldn't know how to behave in a doctor's or lawyer's circle. To them you're a dressmaker, an ignorant creature.' "

IT IS ONE O'CLOCK in the afternoon. Shopping is at its height at the "Nouveaute's de Paris," a drapery establishment in one of the Arcades. There is a monotonous hum of shopmen's voices, the hum one hears at school when the teacher sets the boys to learn something by heart. This regular sound is not interrupted by the laughter of lady customers nor the slam of the glass door, nor the scurrying of the boys.

Polinka, a thin, fair little person whose mother is the head of a dressmaking establishment, is standing in the middle of the shop looking about for someone. A dark-browed boy runs up to her and asks, looking at her very gravely:

41

"What is your pleasure, madam?"

"Nikolai Timofeich always takes my order," answers Polinka.

Nikolai Timofeich, a graceful, dark young man, fashionably dressed, with frizzled hair and a big pin in his cravat, has already cleared a place on the counter and is craning forward, looking at Polinka with a smile.

"Morning, Pelagea Sergeevna!" he cries in a pleasant, hearty baritone voice. "What can I do for you?"

"Good morning!" says Polinka, going up to him. "You see, I'm back again. . . . Show me some gimp, please."

"Gimp—for what purpose?"

"For a bodice trimming—to trim a whole dress, in fact."

"Certainly."

Nikolai Timofeich lays several kinds of gimp before Polinka; she looks at the trimmings listlessly and begins bargaining over them.

"Oh, come, a ruble's not dear," says the shopman persuasively, with a condescending smile. "It's a French trimming, pure silk. . . . We have a commoner sort, if you like, heavier. That's forty-five kopecks a yard; of course, it's nothing like the same quality."

"I want a bead corselet, too, with gimp buttons," says Polinka, bending over the gimp and sighing for some reason. "And have you any bead motifs to match?"

"Yes."

Polinka bends still lower over the counter and asks softly:

"And why did you leave us so early on Thursday, Nikolai Timofeich?"

"Hm! It's queer you noticed it," says the shopman, with a smirk. "You were so taken up with that fine student that . . . it's queer you noticed it!"

Polinka flushes crimson and remains mute. With a nervous quiver in his fingers the shopman closes the boxes, and for no sort of object piles them one on the top of another. A moment of silence follows.

"I want some bead lace, too," says Polinka, lifting her eyes guiltily to the shopman.

"What sort? Black or colored? Bead lace on tulle is the most fashionable trimming."

"And how much is it?"

"The black's from eighty kopecks and the colored from two and a half rubles. I shall never come and see you again," Nikolai Timofeich adds in an undertone.

"Why?"

"Why? It's very simple. You must understand that yourself. Why should I distress myself? It's a queer business! Do you suppose it's a pleasure to me to see that student carrying on with you? I see it all and I understand. Ever since autumn he's been hanging about you and you go for a walk with him almost every day; and when he is with you, you gaze at him as though he were an angel. You are in love with him; there's no one to beat him in your eyes. Well, all right, then, it's no good talking."

Polinka remains mute and moves her finger on the counter in embarrassment.

"I see it all," the shopman goes on. "What inducement have I to come and see you? I've got some pride. It's not everyone likes to play gooseberry. What was it you asked for?"

"Mamma told me to get a lot of things, but I've forgotten. I want some feather trimming too."

"What kind would you like?"

"The best, something fashionable."

"The most fashionable now are real bird feathers. If you want the most fashionable color, it's heliotrope or *kanak*—that is, claret with a yellow shade in it. We have an immense choice. And what all this affair is going to lead to, I really don't understand. Here you are in love, and how is it to end?"

Patches of red come into Nikolai Timofeich's face round his eyes. He crushes the soft feather trimming in his hand and goes on muttering:

"Do you imagine he'll marry you—is that it? You'd better drop any such fancies. Students are forbidden to marry. And do you suppose he comes to see you with honorable intentions? A likely idea! Why, these fine students don't look on us as human beings . . . they only go to see shopkeepers and dressmakers to laugh at their ignorance and to drink. They're ashamed to drink at home and in good houses, but with simple uneducated people like us they don't care what anyone thinks; they'd be ready to stand on their heads. Yes! Well, which feather trimming will you take? And if he hangs about and carries on with you, we know what he is after. . . . When he's a doctor or a lawyer he'll remember you: 'Ah,' he'll say, 'I used to have a pretty fair little thing! I wonder where she is now?' Even now I bet you he boasts among his friends that he's got his eye on a little dressmaker."

Polinka sits down and gazes pensively at the pile of white boxes.

"No, I won't take the feather trimming," she sighs. "Mamma had better choose it for herself; I may get the wrong one. I want six yards of fringe for an overcoat, at forty kopecks the yard. For the same coat I want cocoa-nut buttons, perforated, so they can be sown on firmly. . . ."

Nikolai Timofeich wraps up the fringe and the buttons. She looks at him guiltily and evidently expects him to go on talking, but he remains sullenly silent while he tidies up the feather trimming.

"I mustn't forget some buttons for a dressing-gown . . ." she says after an interval of silence, wiping her pale lips with a handkerchief.

"What kind?"

"It's for a shopkeeper's wife, so give me something rather striking."

"Yes, if it's for a shopkeeper's wife, you'd better have something bright. Here are some buttons. A combination of colors—red, blue, and the fashionable gold shade. Very glaring. The more refined prefer dull black with a bright border. But I don't understand. Can't you see for yourself? What can these . . . walks lead to?"

"I don't know," whispers Polinka, and she bends over the buttons; "I don't know myself what's happening with me, Nikolai Timofeich."

A solid shopman with whiskers forces his way behind Nikolai Timofeich's back, squeezing him to the counter, and beaming with the choicest gallantry, shouts:

"Be so kind, madam, as to step into this department. We have three kinds of jerseys: plain, braided, and trimmed with beads! Which may I have the pleasure of showing you?"

At the same time a stout lady passes by Polinka, pronouncing in a rich, deep voice, almost a bass:

"They must be seamless, with the trademark stamped in them, please."

"Pretend to be looking at the things," Nikolai Timofeich whispers, bending down to Polinka with a forced smile. "Dear me, you do look pale and ill; you are quite changed. He'll throw you over, Pelagea Sergeevna! Or if he does marry you, it won't be for love but from hunger; he'll be tempted by your money. He'll furnish himself a nice home with your dowry, and then be ashamed of you. He'll keep you out of sight of his friends and visitors, because you're uneducated. He'll call you 'my dummy of a wife.' You wouldn't know how to behave in a doctor's or lawyer's circle. To them you're a dressmaker, an ignorant creature."

"Nikolai Timofeich!" somebody shouts from the other end of the shop. "The young lady here wants three yards of ribbon with a metal stripe. Have we any?"

Nikolai Timofeich turns in that direction, smirks, and shouts:

"Yes, we have! Ribbon with a metal stripe, ottoman with a satin stripe, and satin with a moire stripe!"

"Oh, by the way, I mustn't forget, Olga asked me to get her a pair of stays!" says Polinka.

"There are tears in your eyes," says Nikolai Timofeich in dismay. "What's that for? Come to the corset department, I'll screen you—it looks awkward."

With a forced smile and exaggeratedly free and easy manner, the shopman rapidly conducts Polinka to the corset department and conceals her from the public eye behind a high pyramid of boxes.

"What sort of corset may I show you?" he asks aloud, whispering immediately: "Wipe your eyes!"

"I want . . . I want . . . size forty-eight centimeters. Only she wanted one, lined . . . with real whalebone . . . I must talk to you, Nikolai Timofeich. Come today!"

"Talk? What about? There's nothing to talk about."

"You are the only person who . . . cares about me, and I've no one to talk to but you."

"These are not reed or steel, but real whalebone. . . . What is there for us to talk about? It's no use talking. . . . You are going for a walk with him today, I suppose?"

"Yes; I . . . I am."

"Then what's the use of talking? Talk won't help. . . . You are in love, aren't you?"

"Yes . . ." Polinka whispers hesitatingly, and big tears gush from her eyes.

"What is there to say?" mutters Nikolai Timofeich, shrugging his shoulders nervously and turning pale. "There's no need of talk. . . . Wipe your eyes, that's all. I . . . I ask for nothing."

At that moment a tall, lanky shopman comes up to the pyramid of boxes, and says to his customer:

"Let me show you some good elastic garters that do not impede the circulation, certified by medical authority . . ."

Nikolai Timofeich screens Polinka, and, trying to conceal her emotion and his own, wrinkles his face into a smile and says aloud:

"There are two kinds of lace, madam: cotton and silk! Oriental, English, Valenciennes, crochet, torchon, are cotton. And rococo, soutache, Cambray, are silk. . . . For God's sake, wipe your eyes! They're coming this way!"

And seeing that her tears are still gushing he goes on louder than ever:

"Spanish, Rococo, soutache, Cambray . . . stockings, thread, cotton, silk . . ."

VEROCHKA

(*Верочка*, 1887)

*The protagonist Ognev is a guileless, hardworking young man
from the city who, resigned to his lonely bachelor status, has
reveled in his "country life" summer, where he has been befriended
by a rich landowner and his daughter, Vera (familiarly,
Verochka). Dull to passions himself, Ognev is shocked awake by
Verochka's halting confession of love: "These words, so simple
and ordinary, were uttered in ordinary human language, but
Ognev, in acute embarrassment, turned away from Vera, and got
up, while his confusion was followed by terror."*

IVAN ALEXEYVICH OGNEV remembers how on that August evening
he opened the glass door with a rattle and went out on to the
verandah. He was wearing a light Inverness cape and a wide-
brimmed straw hat, the very one that was lying with his top-boots
in the dust under his bed. In one hand he had a big bundle of books
and notebooks, in the other a thick knotted stick.

Behind the door, holding the lamp to show the way, stood the
master of the house, Kuznetsov, a bald old man with a long gray
beard, in a snow-white piqué jacket. The old man was smiling
cordially and nodding his head.

"Goodbye, old fellow!" said Ognev.

Kuznetsov put the lamp on a little table and went out to the
verandah. Two long, narrow shadows moved down the steps
towards the flowerbeds, swayed to and fro, and leaned their heads
on the trunks of the lime-trees.

"Goodbye and once more thank you, my dear fellow!" said Ivan
Alexeyich. "Thank you for your welcome, for your kindness, for

your affection. . . . I shall never forget your hospitality as long as I live. You are so good, and your daughter is so good, and everyone here is so kind, so good-humored and friendly . . . Such a splendid set of people that I don't know how to say what I feel!"

From excess of feeling and under the influence of the home-made wine he had just drunk, Ognev talked in a singing voice like a divinity student, and was so touched that he expressed his feelings not so much by words as by the blinking of his eyes and the twitching of his shoulders. Kuznetsov, who had also drunk a good deal and was touched, craned forward to the young man and kissed him.

"I've grown as fond of you as if I were your dog," Ognev went on. "I've been turning up here almost every day; I've stayed the night a dozen times. It's dreadful to think of all the home-made wine I've drunk. And thank you most of all for your co-operation and help. Without you I should have been busy here over my statistics till October. I shall put in my preface: 'I think it my duty to express my gratitude to the President of the District Zemstvo of N——, Kuznetsov, for his kind co-operation.' There is a brilliant future before statistics! My humble respects to Vera Gavrilovna, and tell the doctors, both the lawyers and your secretary, that I shall never forget their help! And now, old fellow, let us embrace one another and kiss for the last time!"

Ognev, limp with emotion, kissed the old man once more and began going down the steps. On the last step he looked round and asked: "Shall we meet again some day?"

"God knows!" said the old man. "Most likely not!"

"Yes, that's true! Nothing will tempt you to Petersburg and I am never likely to turn up in this district again. Well, goodbye!"

"You had better leave the books behind!" Kuznetsov called after him. "You don't want to drag such a weight with you. I would send them by a servant tomorrow!"

But Ognev was rapidly walking away from the house and was not listening. His heart, warmed by the wine, was brimming over with good-humor, friendliness, and sadness. He walked along thinking how frequently one met with good people, and what a pity it was that nothing was left of those meetings but memories. At times one catches a glimpse of cranes on the horizon, and a faint gust of wind brings their plaintive, ecstatic cry, and a minute later, however greedily one scans the blue distance, one cannot see a speck nor catch a sound; and like that, people with their faces and their words flit through our lives and are drowned in the past, leaving nothing except faint traces in the memory. Having been in the N—— District from the early spring, and having been almost every day at the friendly Kuznetsovs', Ivan Alexeyich had become as much at home with the old man, his daughter, and the servants as though they were his own people; he had grown familiar with the whole house to the smallest detail, with the cozy verandah, the windings of the avenues, the silhouettes of the trees over the kitchen and the bath-house; but as soon as he was out of the gate all this would be changed to memory and would lose its meaning as reality for ever, and in a year or two all these dear images would grow as dim in his consciousness as stories he had read or things he had imagined.

"Nothing in life is so precious as people!" Ognev thought in his emotion, as he strode along the avenue to the gate. "Nothing!"

It was warm and still in the garden. There was a scent of the mignonette, of the tobacco-plants, and of the heliotrope, which were not yet over in the flowerbeds. The spaces between the bushes and the tree-trunks were filled with a fine, soft mist soaked through and through with moonlight, and, as Ognev long remembered, coils of mist that looked like phantoms slowly but perceptibly followed one another across the avenue. The moon stood high above the garden, and below it transparent patches of mist were floating eastward. The whole world seemed to consist of nothing but black silhouettes and wandering white shadows. Ognev, seeing the mist on a moonlight August evening almost for the first time in his life, imagined he was seeing, not nature, but a stage effect in which unskillful workmen, trying to light up the garden with white Bengal fire, hid behind the bushes and let off clouds of white smoke together with the light.

When Ognev reached the garden gate a dark shadow moved away from the low fence and came towards him.

"Vera Gavrilovna!" he said, delighted. "You here? And I have been looking everywhere for you; wanted to say goodbye. . . . Goodbye; I am going away!"

"So early? Why, it's only eleven o'clock."

"Yes, it's time I was off. I have a four-mile walk and then my packing. I must be up early tomorrow."

Before Ognev stood Kuznetsov's daughter Vera, a girl of one-and-twenty, as usual melancholy, carelessly dressed, and attractive. Girls who are dreamy and spend whole days lying down, lazily reading whatever they come across, who are bored and melancholy, are usually careless in their dress. To those of them who have been endowed by nature with taste and an instinct of beauty, the slight carelessness adds a special charm. When Ognev later on remembered her, he could not picture pretty Verochka except in a full blouse which was crumpled in deep folds at the belt and yet did not touch her waist; without her hair done up high and a curl that had come loose from it on her forehead; without the knitted red shawl with ball fringe at the edge which hung disconsolately on Vera's shoulders in the evenings, like a flag on a windless day, and in the daytime lay about, crushed up, in the hall near the men's hats or on a box in the dining-room, where the old cat did not hesitate to sleep on it. This shawl and the folds of her blouse suggested a feeling of freedom and laziness, of good-nature and sitting at home. Perhaps because Vera attracted Ognev he saw in every frill and button something warm, naïve, cozy, something nice and poetical, just what is lacking in cold, insincere women that have no instinct for beauty.

Verochka had a good figure, a regular profile, and beautiful curly hair. Ognev, who had seen few women in his life, thought her a beauty.

"I am going away," he said as he took leave of her at the gate. "Don't remember evil against me! Thank you for everything!"

In the same singing divinity student's voice in which he had talked to her father, with the same blinking and twitching of his shoulders, he began thanking Vera for her hospitality, kindness, and friendliness.

"I've written about you in every letter to my mother," he said. "If everyone were like you and your dad, what a jolly place the world would be! You are such a splendid set of people! All such genuine, friendly people with no nonsense about you."

"Where are you going to now?" asked Vera.

"I am going now to my mother's at Oryol; I shall be a fortnight with her, and then back to Petersburg and work."

"And then?"

"And then? I shall work all the winter and in the spring go somewhere into the provinces again to collect material. Well, be happy, live a hundred years . . . don't remember evil against me. We shall not see each other again."

Ognev stooped down and kissed Vera's hand. Then, in silent emotion, he straightened his cape, shifted his bundle of books to a more comfortable position, paused, and said:

"What a lot of mist!"

"Yes. Have you left anything behind?"

"No, I don't think so. . . ."

For some seconds Ognev stood in silence, then he moved clumsily towards the gate and went out of the garden.

"Stay; I'll see you as far as our wood," said Vera, following him out.

They walked along the road. Now the trees did not obscure the view, and one could see the sky and the distance. As though covered with a veil all nature was hidden in a transparent, colorless haze through which her beauty peeped gaily; where the mist was thicker and whiter it lay heaped unevenly about the stones, stalks, and bushes or drifted in coils over the road, clung close to the earth, and seemed trying not to conceal the view. Through the haze they could see all the road as far as the wood, with dark ditches at the sides and tiny bushes which grew in the ditches and caught the straying wisps of mist. Half a mile from the gate they saw the dark patch of Kuznetsov's wood.

"Why has she come with me? I shall have to see her back," thought Ognev, but looking at her profile he gave a friendly smile and said: "One doesn't want to go away in such lovely weather. It's quite a romantic evening, with the moon, the stillness, and all the etceteras. Do you know, Vera Gavrilovna, here I have lived twenty-nine years in the world and never had a romance. No romantic episode in my whole life, so that I only know by hearsay of rendezvous, 'avenues of sighs,' and kisses. It's not normal! In town, when one sits in one's lodgings, one does not notice the blank, but here in the fresh air one feels it. . . . One resents it!"

"Why is it?"

"I don't know. I suppose I've never had time, or perhaps it was I have never met women who. . . . In fact, I have very few acquaintances and never go anywhere."

For some three hundred paces the young people walked on in silence. Ognev kept glancing at Verochka's bare head and shawl, and days of spring and summer rose to his mind one after another. It had been a period when far from his gray Petersburg lodgings, enjoying the friendly warmth of kind people, nature, and the work he loved, he had not had time to notice how the sunsets followed the glow of dawn, and how, one after another foretelling the end of summer, first the nightingale ceased singing, then the quail, then a little later the landrail. The days slipped by unnoticed, so that life must have been happy and easy. He began calling aloud how reluctantly he, poor and unaccustomed to change of scene and society, had come at the end of April to the N—— District, where he had expected dreariness, loneliness, and indifference to statistics, which he considered was now the foremost among the sciences. When he arrived on an April morning at the little town of N—— he had put up at the inn kept by Ryabukhin, the Old Believer, where for twenty kopecks a day they had given him a light, clean room on condition that he should not smoke indoors. After resting and finding who was the president of the District Zemstvo, he had set off at once on foot to Kuznetsov. He had to walk three miles through lush meadows and young groves. Larks were hovering in the clouds, filling the air with silvery notes, and rooks flapping their wings with sedate dignity floated over the green cornland.

"Good heavens!" Ognev had thought in wonder; "can it be that there's always air like this to breathe here, or is this scent only today, in honor of my coming?"

Expecting a cold, businesslike reception, he went in to Kuznetsov's diffidently, looking up from under his eyebrows and shyly pulling his beard. At first Kuznetsov wrinkled up his brows and could not understand what use the Zemstvo could be to the young man and his statistics; but when the latter explained at length what was material for statistics and how such material was collected, Kuznetsov brightened, smiled, and with childish curiosity began looking at his notebooks. On the evening of the same day Ivan Alexeyich was already sitting at supper with the Kuznetsovs, was rapidly becoming exhilarated by their strong home-made wine, and looking at the calm faces and lazy movements of his new acquaintances, felt all over that sweet, drowsy indolence which makes one want to sleep and stretch and smile; while his new acquaintances looked at him good-naturedly and asked him whether his father and mother were living, how much he earned a month, how often he went to the theater. . . .

Ognev recalled his expeditions about the neighborhood, the picnics, the fishing parties, the visit of the whole party to the convent to see the Mother Superior Marfa, who had given each of the visitors a bead purse; he recalled the hot, endless typically Russian arguments in which the opponents, spluttering and banging the table with their fists, misunderstand and interrupt one another, unconsciously contradict themselves at every phrase, continually change the subject, and after arguing for two or three hours, laugh and say: "Goodness knows what we have been arguing about! Beginning with one thing and going on to another!"

"And do you remember how the doctor and you and I rode to Shestovo?" said Ivan Alexeyich to Vera as they reached the grove. "It was there that the crazy saint met us: I gave him a five-kopeck piece, and he crossed himself three times and flung it into the rye. Good heavens! I am carrying away such a mass of memories that if I could gather them together into a whole it would make a good nugget of gold! I don't understand why clever, perceptive people crowd into Petersburg and Moscow and don't come here. Is there more truth and freedom in the Nevsky and in the big damp houses than here? Really, the idea of artists, scientific men, and journalists all living crowded together in furnished rooms has always seemed to me a mistake."

Twenty paces from the grove the road was crossed by a small narrow bridge with posts at the corners, which had always served as a resting-place for the Kuznetsovs and their guests on their evening walks. From there those who liked could mimic the forest echo, and one could see the road vanish in the dark woodland track.

"Well, here is the bridge!" said Ognev. "Here you must turn back."

Vera stopped and drew a breath.

"Let us sit down," she said, sitting down on one of the posts. "People generally sit down when they say goodbye before starting on a journey."

Ognev settled himself beside her on his bundle of books and went on talking. She was breathless from the walk, and was looking, not at Ivan Alexeyich, but away into the distance so that he could not see her face.

"And what if we meet in ten years' time?" he said. "What shall we be like then? You will be by then the respectable mother of a family, and I shall be the author of some weighty statistical work of no use to anyone, as thick as forty thousand such works. We shall meet and think of old days. . . . Now we are conscious of the present; it absorbs and excites us, but when we meet we shall not remember the day, nor the month, nor even the year in which we saw each other for the last time on this bridge. You will be changed, perhaps. . . . Tell me, will you be different?"

Vera started and turned her face towards him.

"What?" she asked.

"I asked you just now. . . ."

"Excuse me, I did not hear what you were saying."

Only then Ognev noticed a change in Vera. She was pale, breathing fast, and the tremor in her breathing affected her hands and lips and head, and not one curl as usual, but two, came loose and fell on her forehead. . . . Evidently she avoided looking him in the face, and, trying to mask her emotion, at one moment fingered her collar, which seemed to be rasping her neck, at another pulled her red shawl from one shoulder to the other.

"I am afraid you are cold," said Ognev. "It's not at all wise to sit in the mist. Let me see you back to the house."

Vera sat mute.

"What is the matter?" asked Ognev, with a smile. "You sit silent and don't answer my questions. Are you cross, or don't you feel well?"

Vera pressed the palm of her hand to the cheek nearest to Ognev, and then abruptly jerked it away.

"An awful position!" she murmured, with a look of pain on her face. "Awful!"

"How is it awful?" asked Ognev, shrugging his shoulders and not concealing his surprise. "What's the matter?"

Still breathing hard and twitching her shoulders, Vera turned her back to him, looked at the sky for half a minute, and said:

"There is something I must say to you, Ivan Alexeyich. . . ."

"I am listening."

"It may seem strange to you. . . . You will be surprised, but I don't care. . . ."

Ognev shrugged his shoulders once more and prepared himself to listen.

"You see . . ." Verochka began, bowing her head and fingering a ball on the fringe of her shawl. "You see . . . this is what I wanted to tell you. . . . You'll think it strange . . . and silly, but I . . . can't bear it any longer."

Vera's words died away in an indistinct mutter and were suddenly cut short by tears. The girl hid her face in her handkerchief, bent lower than ever, and wept bitterly. Ivan Alexeyich cleared his throat in confusion and looked about him hopelessly, at his wits' end, not knowing what to say or do. Being unused to the sight of tears, he felt his own eyes, too, beginning to smart.

"Well, what next!" he muttered helplessly. "Vera Gavrilovna, what's this for, I should like to know? My dear girl, are you . . . are

you ill? Or has someone been nasty to you? Tell me, perhaps I
could, so to say . . . help you. . . ."

When, trying to console her, he ventured cautiously to remove
her hands from her face, she smiled at him through her tears and said:

"I . . . love you!"

These words, so simple and ordinary, were uttered in ordinary
human language, but Ognev, in acute embarrassment, turned away
from Vera, and got up, while his confusion was followed by terror.

The sad, warm, sentimental mood induced by leave-taking and
the home-made wine suddenly vanished, and gave place to an acute
and unpleasant feeling of awkwardness. He felt an inward revulsion;
he looked askance at Vera, and now that by declaring her love for
him she had cast off the aloofness which so adds to a woman's charm,
she seemed to him, as it were, shorter, plainer, more ordinary.

"What's the meaning of it?" he thought with horror. "But I . . .
do I love her or not? That's the question!"

And she breathed easily and freely now that the worst and most
difficult thing was said. She, too, got up, and looking Ivan
Alexeyich straight in the face, began talking rapidly, warmly,
irrepressibly.

As a man suddenly panic-stricken cannot afterwards remember
the succession of sounds accompanying the catastrophe that
overwhelmed him, so Ognev cannot remember Vera's words and
phrases. He can only recall the meaning of what she said, and the
sensation her words evoked in him. He remembers her voice,
which seemed stifled and husky with emotion, and the extraordinary
music and passion of her intonation. Laughing, crying with tears
glistening on her eyelashes, she told him that from the first day of
their acquaintance he had struck her by his originality, his
intelligence, his kind, intelligent eyes, by his work and objects in
life; that she loved him passionately, deeply, madly; that when
coming into the house from the garden in the summer she saw his
cape in the hall or heard his voice in the distance, she felt a cold
shudder at her heart, a foreboding of happiness; even his slightest
jokes had made her laugh; in every figure in his note-books she saw
something extraordinarily wise and grand; his knotted stick seemed
to her more beautiful than the trees.

The grove and the wisps of mist and the black ditches at the side
of the road seemed hushed listening to her, while something
strange and unpleasant was passing in Ognev's heart. . . . Telling
him of her love, Vera was enchantingly beautiful; she spoke

eloquently and passionately, but he felt neither pleasure nor gladness, as he would have liked to; he felt nothing but compassion for Vera, pity and regret that a good girl should be distressed on his account. Whether he was affected by generalizations from reading or by the insuperable habit of looking at things objectively, which so often hinders people from living, but Vera's ecstasies and suffering struck him as affected, not to be taken seriously, and at the same time rebellious feeling whispered to him that all he was hearing and seeing now, from the point of view of nature and personal happiness, was more important than any statistics and books and truths. . . . And he raged and blamed himself, though he did not understand exactly where he was in fault.

To complete his embarrassment, he was absolutely at a loss what to say, and yet something he must say. To say bluntly, "I don't love you," was beyond him, and he could not bring himself to say "Yes," because however much he rummaged in his heart he could not find one spark of feeling in it. . . .

He was silent, and she meanwhile was saying that for her there was no greater happiness than to see him, to follow him wherever he liked this very moment, to be his wife and helper, and that if he went away from her she would die of misery.

"I cannot stay here!" she said, wringing her hands. "I am sick of the house and this wood and the air. I cannot bear the everlasting peace and aimless life, I can't endure our colorless, pale people, who are all as like one another as two drops of water! They are all good-natured and warm-hearted because they are all well-fed and know nothing of struggle or suffering, . . . I want to be in those big damp houses where people suffer, embittered by work and need. . . ."

And this, too, seemed to Ognev affected and not to be taken seriously. When Vera had finished he still did not know what to say, but it was impossible to be silent, and he muttered:

"Vera Gavrilovna, I am very grateful to you, though I feel I've done nothing to deserve such . . . feeling . . . on your part. Besides, as an honest man I ought to tell you that . . . happiness depends on equality—that is, when both parties are . . . equally in love. . . ."

But he was immediately ashamed of his mutterings and ceased. He felt that his face at that moment looked stupid, guilty, blank, that it was strained and affected. . . . Vera must have been able to read the truth on his countenance, for she suddenly became grave, turned pale, and bent her head.

"You must forgive me," Ognev muttered, not able to endure the silence. "I respect you so much that . . . it pains me. . . ."

Vera turned sharply and walked rapidly homewards. Ognev followed her.

"No, don't!" said Vera, with a wave of her hand. "Don't come; I can go alone."

"Oh, yes . . . I must see you home anyway."

Whatever Ognev said, it all to the last word struck him as loathsome and flat. The feeling of guilt grew greater at every step. He raged inwardly, clenched his fists, and cursed his coldness and his stupidity with women. Trying to stir his feelings, he looked at Verochka's beautiful figure, at her hair and the traces of her little feet on the dusty road; he remembered her words and her tears, but all that only touched his heart and did not quicken his pulse.

"Ach! one can't force oneself to love," he assured himself, and at the same time he thought, "But shall I ever fall in love without? I am nearly thirty! I have never met anyone better than Vera and I never shall. . . . Oh, this premature old age! Old age at thirty!"

Vera walked on in front more and more rapidly, without looking back at him or raising her head. It seemed to him that sorrow had made her thinner and narrower in the shoulders.

"I can imagine what's going on in her heart now!" he thought, looking at her back. "She must be ready to die with shame and mortification! My God, there's so much life, poetry, and meaning in it that it would move a stone, and I . . . I am stupid and absurd!"[1]

At the gate Vera stole a glance at him, and, shrugging and wrapping her shawl round her, walked rapidly away down the avenue.

Ivan Alexeyich was left alone. Going back to the grove, he walked slowly, continually standing still and looking round at the gate with an expression in his whole figure that suggested that he could not believe his own memory. He looked for Vera's footprints on the road, and could not believe that the girl who had so attracted him had just declared her love, and that he had so clumsily and bluntly "refused" her. For the first time in his life it was his lot to learn by experience how little that a man does depends on his own will, and to suffer in his own person the feelings of a decent, kindly man who has against his will caused his neighbor cruel, undeserved anguish.

---

[1] Chekhov, in the story's final publication in his *Collected Works*, deleted these painful sentences: "*Listen, Vera Gavrilovna!*" and *against his will he suddenly let out a shriek.* "*Don't begin to think that I . . . that I . . . .*" *Ognev hesitated and fell silent.*

His conscience tormented him, and when Vera disappeared he felt as though he had lost something very precious, something very near and dear which he could never find again. He felt that with Vera a part of his youth had slipped away from him, and that the moments which he had passed through so fruitlessly would never be repeated.

When he reached the bridge he stopped and sank into thought. He wanted to discover the reason of his strange coldness. That it was due to something within him and not outside himself was clear to him. He frankly acknowledged to himself that it was not the intellectual coldness of which clever people so often boast, not the coldness of a conceited fool, but simply impotence of soul, incapacity for being moved by beauty, premature old age brought on by education, his casual existence, struggling for a livelihood, his homeless life in lodgings. From the bridge he walked slowly, as it were reluctantly, into the wood. Here, where in the dense black darkness glaring patches of moonlight gleamed here and there, where he felt nothing except his thoughts, he longed passionately to regain what he had lost.

And Ivan Alexeyich remembers that he went back again. Urging himself on with his memories, forcing himself to picture Vera, he strode rapidly towards the garden. There was no mist by then along the road or in the garden, and the bright moon looked down from the sky as though it had just been washed; only the eastern sky was dark and misty. . . . Ognev remembers his cautious steps, the dark windows, the heavy scent of heliotrope and mignonette. His old friend Karo, wagging his tail amicably, came up to him and sniffed his hand. This was the one living creature who saw him walk two or three times round the house, stand near Vera's dark window, and with a deep sigh and a wave of his hand walk out of the garden.

An hour later he was in the town, and, worn out and exhausted, leaned his body and hot face against the gatepost of the inn as he knocked at the gate. Somewhere in the town a dog barked sleepily, and as though in response to his knock, someone clanged the hour on an iron plate near the church.

"You prowl about at night," grumbled his host, the Old Believer, opening the door to him, in a long nightgown like a woman's. "You had better be saying your prayers instead of prowling about."

When Ivan Alexeyich reached his room he sank on the bed and gazed a long, long time at the light. Then he tossed his head and began packing.

THE BEAUTIES

(*Красавицы*, 1888)

This love story is an unusually essay-like two-part narrative. In the first episode, Chekhov is perhaps recalling details of a journey he took as a teenager with his grandfather on the southern steppe. At a stop to see a friend of his grandfather's, the boy is stunned by the beauty of a teenaged girl: "Sitting at the table, I looked in the girl's face as she gave me the glass, and I suddenly felt a breeze run through my soul and blow away all the day's impressions of boredom and dust. I saw the enchanting features of the most beautiful of faces I have ever encountered in real life or in dreams. Before me stood a beauty and I understood this from a glance in the same way I understand lightning."

The novelist Philip Pullman describes "The Beauties" in a way that Chekhov might have appreciated: "It's a story in which nothing happens, twice." I have included as footnotes Chekhov's two longest deletions from the original journal publication; they change nothing but add a few sparkling details. I acknowledge the help of Paul Richardson, editor of Russian Life *magazine, who corrected and improved my translation before its publication in 2020.*

I

I REMEMBER WHEN I was still in high school in the fifth or sixth level, I traveled with my grandfather from the village of Bolshaya Krepkaya in the Don region to Rostov-on-Don. It was a sultry, oppressive, boring August day. Out of the heat and dryness, a scorching wind drove a cloud of dust to meet us, gluing our eyes together, parching our mouths. You didn't want to look around or speak or think, and when the drowsy driver, the Ukrainian Karpo, waving at the horse, lashed my peaked cap with his whip, I did not protest or let out a sound, but only roused up from a half-sleep and despondently and meekly looked in the distance to see if I could glimpse the village through the dust. We stopped to feed the horses in the big Armenian village of Bakhchi-Salakh, at a rich Armenian's my grandfather knew.

Never in my life have I seen such a caricature of an Armenian. Picture a small, close-cut head with bushy, low-hanging brows, a hawk-nose with a long, gray moustache and a wide mouth, from which jutted out the long cherrywood mouthpiece of a Turkish pipe. This little head was awkwardly stuck atop a lean, humpbacked body, dressed in a fantastic costume: a short, red jacket and wide, bright-blue, loose trousers. This figure walked legs spread apart and shuffling in his slippers; and he spoke without taking the pipe out of his mouth, holding himself apart with pure Armenian dignity: not smiling, his eyes bulging, and trying to give his guests as little attention as possible.

In the Armenian's rooms there was neither a breeze nor dust, but it was for all that as unpleasant, stuffy, and dreary as on the steppes or along the road. I remember, dusty and worn out by the heat, I sat in the corner on a green chest. The unpainted wooden walls, furniture, and ochre-stained floors gave off the smells of dry, sunbaked wood. No matter where you looked, there were flies, flies, flies.

In low voices, Grandfather and the Armenian spoke about pasturing, manure, sheep. . . . I knew that the samovar would take a whole hour to heat up, that Grandfather would drink tea for at least an hour, that then he would lie down and sleep two or three hours, and that I had a quarter of a day of anticipating leaving, after which there would again be the heat, dust, and jolting roads. Listening to the muttering of the two voices, it began to seem to me that I had for a long, long time been watching the Armenian, the cupboard with dishes, the flies, the windows, through which beat the hot sun, and that I would cease watching them only in the very distant future, and a hatred for the steppes, the sun, and the flies overwhelmed me.

A Ukrainian woman in a kerchief brought in a tray of dishes, and then a samovar. The Armenian unhurriedly went into the entryway and called out: "Mashya! Come in and pour the tea! Where are you? Mashya!"

Hurried steps were heard, and into the room came a girl of about sixteen in a simple cotton dress and white kerchief. Washing off the dishes and pouring the tea, she stood with her back to me, and I only noticed that she was thin at the waist, barefoot, and that her little heels were naked under her loose, tied-at-the-ankles trousers.

Our host invited me to drink tea. Sitting at the table, I looked in the girl's face as she gave me the glass, and I suddenly felt a breeze run through my soul and blow away all the day's impressions of boredom and dust. I saw the enchanting features of the most beautiful of faces I have ever encountered in real life or in dreams. Before me stood a beauty and I understood this from a glance in the same way I understand lightning.

I am prepared to swear that Masha, or Mashya, as her father called her, was a genuine beauty, but I can't prove this. Sometimes it happens that clouds huddle in a disorderly way on the horizon and the sun, hiding behind them, paints them and the sky in all the colors: purple, orange, gold, violet, muddy-pink; one little cloud resembles a monk, another a fish, a third a Turk in a turban. The sunset, having enveloped three clouds, shines on the church-cross, on the windows of the manor house, reflects in the river and pools, flickers on the trees; far away against a distant sunsetting background, a flock of wild ducks flies somewhere to spend the night. . . . And a herder-boy driving his cows, a surveyor going in his carriage across a dam, and landowners out strolling—everyone looks at the sunset and every last one finds it terribly beautiful, but no one knows or can say what its beauty consists of.

I was not alone in finding the Armenian girl beautiful. My grandfather, a gruff old man of eighty, indifferent to women and the beauties of nature, tenderly gazed at Masha for a whole minute and asked, "This is your daughter, Avet Nazarych?"

"Yes, she's my daughter," answered our host.

"A fine young lady," praised grandfather.

An artist might call the Armenian girl's beauty classical and severe. It was just that sort of beauty, the contemplation of which, from God knows where, inspires in you the conviction that you are seeing the exactly right features, that the hair, eyes, nose, mouth, neck, chest and every single movement of a young body have been brought together in one complete harmonious accord in which nature has not made a single mistake in the smallest detail; it seems to you the ideal of a beautiful woman must have such a nose as Masha has, straight, with a small crook, just such dark, big eyes, just such long lashes, just such a listless look, that her black, curly hair and brows go just right with the delicate, fair forehead and cheeks, as green reeds do in a quiet stream; Masha's white neck and youthful chest are barely developed, but to sculpt them successfully, it seems you would need to command the most tremendous creative talent. You look, and little by little comes to you the desire to say to Masha something unusually pleasant, sincere, beautiful, as beautiful as she herself is.

At first I was hurt and ashamed that Masha did not turn any attention at all to me and looked down the whole time; some kind of special atmosphere, it seemed to me, happy and proud, separated her from me and jealously hid her from my glances.

"It's because," I thought, "I'm completely dusty and sunburned—that I'm still a boy."

But then little by little I forgot about myself and completely surrendered myself to the consciousness of beauty. I no longer remembered about the steppes' boredom, about the dust, no longer heard the buzz of the flies or took in the taste of the tea, and only felt that across the table from me stood a beautiful girl.

I was conscious of this beauty in a strange way. There was neither desire nor excitement, and Masha did not stir pleasure but a heavy, although pleasant, sadness in me. This sadness was vague, hazy, like a dream. Somehow I felt sorry for myself, and for my grandfather, for the Armenian, and even for the Armenian girl. It felt as if we four had lost something important and necessary for life, which we would never again find. Grandfather also became sad. He spoke no more about threshing or sheep but was silent and pensively looked at Masha.[1]

After tea Grandfather lay down to sleep, and I left the house and sat on the porch. The house, like all houses in Bakhchi-Salakh, stood on an exposed sunny place; there were no trees, no awnings, no shade. The Armenian's big yard, overgrown with pigweed and mallow, was, despite the strong heat, lively and bright. Over one of the low wattle fences that intersected the big yard here and there,

---

[1] At this point in the original publication in the magazine *New Times*, Chekhov wrote: *"Our silence did not seem awkward because our host was silent himself. He knew his daughter was beautiful. In reply to our silence, he somehow awkwardly grunted and his face expressed: 'She's very beautiful and unusual, but we will make as if we don't notice this.'"*

threshing was going on. Twelve horses, harnessed in a row and
turning in one long radius, ran round a post driven into the very
middle of the threshing floor. Alongside walked a Ukrainian in a
long jacket and wide pants, cracking a whip and crying out in a
tone that suggested he wanted to taunt the horses and brag of his
power over them.

"Yah! You cursed ones! Yah! Cholera take you!—Afraid?"[2]

The horses—reddish-brown, white, and spotted—not understanding why they were being made to run around in circles in one
place and stamp wheat-straw, reluctantly ran at their utmost
strength and, affronted, flicked their tails. From under their hooves
a wind raised whole clouds of golden chaff and carried it far beyond
the fence. Around the tall, fresh hayricks, women bustled with
rakes, and carts moved along; beyond the hayricks in another yard,
another dozen such horses ran around another post, and another
identical Ukrainian cracked his whip and jeered at his horses.

The steps I was sitting on were hot; sap oozed from the thin
hand-rails and window frames; under the steps and under the
shutters in the strips of shadow red bugs huddled together. The sun
baked me on the head and on the chest and on my back, but I did
not mind this and only sensed how, behind me on the porch, and
in the rooms on the plank floor, bare feet were pattering. Fetching
away the tea dishes, Masha ran down the steps, making a breeze on
me, and like a bird, she was flying to a small, sooty outbuilding,
probably a kitchen, from which came the smell of roast lamb and
the sounds of an angry Armenian conversation. She disappeared
into the dark doorway and on the threshold there appeared, instead
of her, an old, bent Armenian woman with a red face and in green
trousers. The old woman was angry and was scolding somebody.
Soon, on the threshold, Masha appeared, reddened from the
kitchen heat, with a big loaf of black bread on her shoulder.
Beautifully bending under the heavy bread, she ran through the
yard to the threshing-floor; she hopped over the fence and,

---

[2] Here, in the original publication, Chekhov wrote: "*The Armenian left the house,
spreading his feet, went down past me on the stairs and, not taking the pipe out of his
mouth, tossed out some kind of sneezy sounds, of this kind, 'Tkhan-mkhachkha!' Masha
ran to him and he began telling her something quickly and angrily—probably a rebuke. She,
silently and lowering her eyes, listened to him, then ran into the kitchen, from there then
to the barn, and I again saw how the Ukrainian stopped yelling and cracking his stick and
followed her with his eyes.*"

plunging into the cloud of golden chaff, she disappeared beyond the carts. The Ukrainian who was driving the horses lowered his lash, went quiet, and for a minute silently looked towards the carts, and then, when the Armenian girl again flitted by, around the horses, and hopped across the fence, he followed her with his eyes and cried out at the horses in such a tone as if he were angry:

"To hell with you, you evil ones!"

And the whole time then I listened to her never-stopping bare feet; I saw how, with a serious, anxious face, she rushed through the yard. She ran now down the steps, enveloping me in a breeze; now into the kitchen, now to the threshing floor, now beyond the gates, and I was barely able to turn my head to keep up with her.

The more often she flashed before my eyes with her beauty, the stronger became my sadness. I was sorry for myself, for her, for the Ukrainian, who sadly followed her with his glance every time she ran through the cloud of chaff to the carts. Whether I envied her beauty or I pitied myself that the girl wasn't mine and never would be, and that I, for her, was a stranger, or that I vaguely felt that her rare beauty was an accident and not a necessity and, like everything on earth, not long-lasting, or whether my sadness was the special feeling excited by the contemplation of supreme beauty, God knows.

Hours of waiting passed by unnoticed. It seemed to me that I had not had enough time to look at Masha when Karpo rode down to the river and bathed the horse and now began to harness it. The wet horse snorted with pleasure and knocked its hooves against the shafts. Karpo cried at her, "Back—back!" Grandfather woke up.

Masha opened the creaking gates for us. We sat down in the cart and left the yard. We went in silence, as if angry at one another.

When in two or three hours Rostov and Nakhichevan appeared in the distance, Karpo, having been silent the whole time, quickly looked around and said, "What a fine one, the Armenian's girl!" and he gave the horse a lash.

II

Another time, having become a university student, I was on the railroad going south. It was May. At one of the stations, I think between Belgorod and Kharkov, I got out of the carriage to take a stroll along the platform.

Evening shadows already lay on the station garden, on the platform, and on the fields. The train station blocked the sunset, but as the breezy puffs of smoke coming from the engine were painted in tender pink light, it was apparent that the sun had not yet vanished.

Walking up and down the platform, I noticed that the majority of the strolling passengers went and stood only around one second-class carriage, and with such expressions as if in this carriage sat some famous person. In the midst of the curious whom I encountered near this carriage, I found my fellow-traveler, an artillery officer: young, smart, warm, and sympathetic, as everyone is whom one gets to know on the road by chance and for not too long.

"What are you looking at there?" I asked.

He didn't answer and only pointed out to me with his eyes a female figure. It was a very young girl, seventeen or eighteen, dressed in Russian style, with an uncovered head and with a little cape carelessly thrown over one shoulder. She was not a passenger, but must have been a daughter or sister of the stationmaster. She stood near the carriage window and was speaking with some elderly female passenger. Before I had time to realize what I was seeing, I was overcome suddenly by the feeling that I had once experienced in the Armenian village.

The girl was a remarkable beauty, and as to this neither I nor any of those together with me who looked at her had any doubts.

If, as is the custom, her appearance was described bit by bit, what was really beautiful about her was only her blond, wavy, thick hair, let loose and with a black ribbon tied up on her head; all the rest was either irregular or just very ordinary. Whether from her particular manner of coquetting or from being nearsighted, her eyes were scrunched up, her nose was uncertainly turned up, she had a small mouth, a weak profile vapidly drawn, shoulders slender for her age, but nonetheless the girl produced the impression of genuine beauty, and looking at her I was convinced that the Russian face, in order to seem beautiful, does not need to have strictly correct features, and besides, if the girl instead of a tilted nose presented a different one—correct and flawless in form like the Armenian girl's—it seemed to me that all the charm of her face would have been lost.

Standing by the window and conversing, the girl, shivering from the evening dampness, occasionally looked around at us, now standing with hands on her hips, now raising her hands to her head in order to fix her hair; she spoke, laughed. She depicted on her face now amazement, now horror, and I don't remember that at any instant her body and face were at peace; the whole secret and magic of her beauty was contained especially in those little, unceasing, elegant movements: in her smile, in the play of her face, in her quick glances at us, in the blend of delicate grace of those movements with youthfulness and freshness and the frankness of the sounds of her laughter and voice, and with that fragility that we so love in children, in birds, in young deer and young trees.

This was the butterfly-like beauty of waltzing, fluttering through a garden, laughter, joyousness; it does not get tied up by serious thoughts, sadness, and repose, and it seemed only a good wind would be needed to rush along the platform or for it to rain in order for the fragile body to fade suddenly and her capricious beauty to scatter like pollen.

"Just so," the officer muttered with a sigh when after the second bell we were setting off for our carriage.

But what that "Just so" meant I won't undertake to say. Perhaps he was sad and didn't want to leave the beauty and the spring evening to go inside the stuffy carriage or, perhaps, like me, he was unaccountably sorry for the beauty, for himself and me, for all the passengers, who listlessly, reluctantly wandered back to our carriages. As we walked past the station window, a pale, red-headed telegrapher with high curls and a washed-out, broad-cheeked face was sitting behind the apparatus, and the officer sighed and said, "I'll bet this telegrapher is in love with that pretty thing. To live in the country, under one roof with such an ethereal creature and not fall in love—that's beyond the strength of anyone. But, my friend, what a misfortune, what kind of mockery is it to be a hunched, ragged, dull, respectable, and not-stupid person, and be in love with this stupid, pretty girl who pays you no attention! Or even worse, imagine that this telegrapher is in love *and* married, and that his wife is as hunched, ragged, and respectable a person as he is himself—torture!"

Near our carriage, leaning on his elbows on the railing of the platform, stood the conductor looking towards where the beauty stood, and his haggard, wrinkled, unpleasantly meaty face, weary from sleepless nights and the jostling carriage, expressed a tenderness and the deepest sadness, as if in the girl he saw his youth, happiness, his sobriety, purity, wife, and children, as if he were repenting and felt with his whole existence that this girl was not his, and that for him, the happiness of an ordinary human passenger, due to his premature old age, uncouthness, and fat face, was as far away as heaven.

The third bell struck, whistles blew, and the train lazily started off. Through our windows first of all flitted by the conductor, the station-master, and then the garden and the beauty with her odd, sly, childish smile.

Sticking my head out and looking back, I saw how she, following the train with her eyes, proceeded along the platform past the window where the telegrapher was sitting; she fixed her hair and ran into the garden. The station no longer shut off the west, the countryside was open, but the sun had already set, and the black puffs of smoke drifted over the green, velvety crops. It was sad: in the spring air, in the darkening sky, and in the carriage.

Our conductor entered the carriage and began lighting the candles.

THE NAME-DAY PARTY

(*Именины*, 1888)

Sometimes known as "The Party" or "The Birthday Party" in English translations, the Russian name-day party is celebrated similarly to a birthday party, but denotes the saint's day associated with a particular person's name, in this case, Pyotr (or Peter).

Chekhov rarely admired his own work, but he was very proud of one aspect of this story. He wrote to his close friend and confided: "I satisfied the women with 'The Name-Day Party.' Wherever I go, they praise it all around. Truly, it's not bad to be a doctor and understand what you're writing about. The ladies say the childbirth is described correctly."[1]

This is the only story in the anthology depicting the love, strained though it may be, of a married couple: "Olga Mikhalovna came to herself. She was suddenly aware of her passionate love for this man, remembered that he was her husband, Pyotr Dmitrich, without whom she could not live for a day, and who loved her passionately, too." In its various editions, Chekhov wrestled with the shape of the story, eventually deleting several pages from the middle. He reflected on its composition to his friend: "I would gladly describe all of my hero, describe him with feeling, understanding, and deliberation. I'd describe his emotions while his wife was in labor. . . . I'd describe the midwife and doctors having tea in the middle of the night, I'd describe the rain. . . . It would be sheer pleasure for me, because I love digging deep and rummaging. But what can I do? I began the story on September 10th with the thought that I have to

---

[1] Letter to Alexei Suvorin, 15 November 1888 [my translation].

finish it by October 5th at the latest; if I miss the deadline I'll be going back on my word and will be left without any money."[2] I have included as a footnote one short passage near the end about those "emotions" of Pyotr Dmitrich's that Chekhov deleted in the final edition.

I

AFTER THE FESTIVE dinner with its eight courses and its endless conversation, Olga Mikhalovna, whose husband's name-day was being celebrated, went out into the garden. The duty of smiling and talking incessantly, the clatter of the crockery, the stupidity of the servants, the long intervals between the courses, and the stays she had put on to conceal her condition from the visitors, wearied her to exhaustion. She longed to get away from the house, to sit in the shade and rest her heart with thoughts of the baby which was to be born to her in another two months. She was used to these thoughts coming to her as she turned to the left out of the big avenue into the narrow path. Here in the thick shade of the plums and cherry-trees the dry branches used to scratch her neck and shoulders; a spider's web would settle on her face, and there would rise up in her mind the image of a little creature of undetermined sex and undefined features, and it began to seem as though it were not the spider's web that tickled her face and neck caressingly, but that little creature. When, at the end of the path, a thin wicker hurdle came into sight, and behind it podgy beehives with tiled roofs; when in the motionless, stagnant air there came a smell of hay and honey, and a soft buzzing of bees was audible, then the little creature would take complete possession of Olga Mikhalovna. She used to sit down on a bench near the shanty woven of branches, and fall to thinking.

This time, too, she went on as far as the seat, sat down, and began thinking; but instead of the little creature there rose up in her imagination the figures of the grown-up people whom she had just left. She felt dreadfully uneasy that she, the hostess, had deserted her

---

[2] Letter to Alexei Suvorin, 27 October 1888, in *Anton Chekhov's Life and Thought*, trans. Michael Henry Heim and Simon Karlinsky (Berkeley: University of California Press, 1975), 117–18.

guests, and she remembered how her husband, Pyotr Dmitrich, and her uncle, Nikolai Nikolaich, had argued at dinner about trial by jury, about the press, and about the higher education of women. Her husband, as usual, argued in order to show off his Conservative ideas before his visitors—and still more in order to disagree with her uncle, whom he disliked. Her uncle contradicted him and wrangled over every word he uttered, so as to show the company that he, Uncle Nikolai Nikolaich, still retained his youthful freshness of spirit and free-thinking in spite of his fifty-nine years. And towards the end of dinner even Olga Mikhalovna herself could not resist taking part and unskillfully attempting to defend university education for women—not that that education stood in need of her defense, but simply because she wanted to annoy her husband, who to her mind was unfair. The guests were wearied by this discussion, but they all thought it necessary to take part in it, and talked a great deal, although none of them took any interest in trial by jury or the higher education of women. . . .

Olga Mikhalovna was sitting on the nearest side of the hurdle near the shanty. The sun was hidden behind the clouds. The trees and the air were overcast as before rain, but in spite of that it was hot and stifling. The hay cut under the trees on the previous day was lying ungathered, looking melancholy, with here and there a patch of color from the faded flowers, and from it came a heavy, sickly scent. It was still. The other side of the hurdle there was a monotonous hum of bees. . . .

Suddenly she heard footsteps and voices; someone was coming along the path towards the beehouse.

"How stifling it is!" said a feminine voice. "What do you think—is it going to rain, or not?"

"It is going to rain, my charmer, but not before night," a very familiar male voice answered listlessly. "There will be a good rain."

Olga Mikhalovna calculated that if she made haste to hide in the shanty they would pass by without seeing her, and she would not have to talk and to force herself to smile. She picked up her skirts, bent down and crept into the shanty. At once she felt upon her face, her neck, her arms, the hot air as heavy as steam. If it had not been for the stuffiness and the close smell of rye bread, fennel, and brushwood, which prevented her from breathing freely, it would have been delightful to hide from her visitors here under the thatched roof in the dusk, and to think about the little creature. It was cozy and quiet.

"What a pretty spot!" said a feminine voice. "Let us sit here, Pyotr Dmitrich."

Olga Mikhalovna began peeping through a crack between two branches. She saw her husband, Pyotr Dmitrich, and Lubochka Sheller, a girl of seventeen who had not long left boarding-school. Pyotr Dmitrich, with his hat on the back of his head, listless and indolent from having drunk so much at the luncheon, slouched by the hurdle and raked the hay into a heap with his foot; Lubochka, pink with the heat and pretty as ever, stood with her hands behind her, watching the lazy movements of his big, handsome person.

Olga Mikhalovna knew that her husband was attractive to women, and did not like to see him with them. There was nothing out of the way in Pyotr Dmitrich's lazily raking together the hay in order to sit down on it with Lubochka and chatter to her of trivialities; there was nothing out of the way, either, in pretty Lubochka's looking at him with her soft eyes; but yet Olga Mikhalovna felt vexed with her husband and frightened and pleased that she could listen to them.

"Sit down, enchantress," said Pyotr Dmitrich, sinking down on the hay and stretching. "That's right. Come, tell me something."

"What next! If I begin telling you anything you will go to sleep."

"Me go to sleep? Allah forbid! Can I go to sleep while eyes like yours are watching me?"

In her husband's words, and in the fact that he was lolling with his hat on the back of his head in the presence of a lady, there was nothing out of the way either. He was spoilt by women, knew that they found him attractive, and had adopted with them a special tone which everyone said suited him. With Lubochka he behaved as with all women. But, all the same, Olga Mikhalovna was jealous.

"Tell me, please," said Lubochka, after a brief silence—"is it true that you are to be tried for something?"

"I? Yes, I am . . . numbered among the transgressors, my charmer."

"But what for?"

"For nothing, but just . . . it's chiefly a question of politics," yawned Pyotr Dmitrich—"the antagonisms of Left and Right. I, an obscurantist and reactionary, ventured in an official paper to make use of an expression offensive in the eyes of such immaculate Gladstones as Vladimir Pavlovich Vladimirov and our local justice of the peace—Kuzma Grigorich Vostryakov."

Pytor Dmitrich yawned again and went on:

"And it is the way with us that you may express disapproval of the sun or the moon, or anything you like, but God preserve you from touching the Liberals! Heaven forbid! A Liberal is like the poisonous dry fungus which covers you with a cloud of dust if you accidentally touch it with your finger."

"What happened to you?"

"Nothing particular. The whole flare-up started from the merest trifle. A teacher, a detestable person of clerical associations, hands to Vostryakov a petition against a tavern-keeper, charging him with insulting language and behavior in a public place. Everything showed that both the teacher and the tavern-keeper were drunk as cobblers, and that they behaved equally badly. If there had been insulting behavior, the insult had anyway been mutual. Vostryakov ought to have fined them both for a breach of the peace and have turned them out of the court—that is all. But that's not our way of doing things. With us what stands first is not the person—not the fact itself, but the trade-mark and label. However great a rascal a teacher may be, he is always in the right because he is a teacher; a tavern-keeper is always in the wrong because he is a tavern-keeper and a money-grubber. Vostryakov placed the tavern-keeper under arrest. The man appealed to the Circuit Court; the Circuit Court triumphantly upheld Vostryakov's decision. Well, I stuck to my own opinion. . . . Got a little hot. . . . That was all."

Pyotr Dmitrich spoke calmly with careless irony. In reality the trial that was hanging over him worried him extremely. Olga Mikhalovna remembered how on his return from the unfortunate session he had tried to conceal from his household how troubled he was, and how dissatisfied with himself. As an intelligent man he could not help feeling that he had gone too far in expressing his disagreement; and how much lying had been needful to conceal that feeling from himself and from others! How many unnecessary conversations there had been! How much grumbling and insincere laughter at what was not laughable! When he learned that he was to be brought up before the Court, he seemed at once harassed and depressed; he began to sleep badly, stood oftener than ever at the windows, drumming on the panes with his fingers. And he was ashamed to let his wife see that he was worried, and it vexed her.

"They say you have been in the province of Poltava?" Lubochka questioned him.

"Yes," answered Pyotr Dmitrich. "I came back the day before yesterday."

"I expect it is very nice there."

"Yes, it is very nice, very nice indeed; in fact, I arrived just in time for the haymaking, I must tell you, and in the Ukraine the haymaking is the most poetical moment of the year. Here we have a big house, a big garden, a lot of servants, and a lot going on, so that you don't see the haymaking; here it all passes unnoticed. There, at the farm, I have a meadow of forty-five acres as flat as my hand. You can see the men mowing from any window you stand at. They are mowing in the meadow, they are mowing in the garden. There are no visitors, no fuss nor hurry either, so that you can't help seeing, feeling, hearing nothing but the haymaking. There is a smell of hay indoors and outdoors. There's the sound of the scythes from sunrise to sunset. Altogether Little Russia is a charming country. Would you believe it, when I was drinking water from the rustic wells and filthy vodka in some Jew's tavern, when on quiet evenings the strains of the Little Russian fiddle and the tambourines reached me, I was tempted by a fascinating idea— to settle down on my place and live there as long as I chose, far away from Circuit Courts, intellectual conversations, philosophizing women, long dinners. . . ."

Pyotr Dmitrich was not lying. He was unhappy and really longed to rest. And he had visited his Poltava property simply to avoid seeing his study, his servants, his acquaintances, and everything that could remind him of his wounded vanity and his mistakes.

Lubochka suddenly jumped up and waved her hands about in horror.

"Oh! A bee, a bee!" she shrieked. "It will sting!"

"Nonsense; it won't sting," said Pyotr Dmitrich. "What a coward you are!"

"No, no, no," cried Lubochka; and looking round at the bees, she walked rapidly back.

Pyotr Dmitrich walked away after her, looking at her with a softened and melancholy face. He was probably thinking, as he looked at her, of his farm, of solitude, and—who knows?—perhaps he was even thinking how snug and cozy life would be at the farm if his wife had been this girl—young, pure, fresh, not corrupted by higher education, not with child. . . .

When the sound of their footsteps had died away, Olga Mikhalovna came out of the shanty and turned towards the house.

She wanted to cry. She was by now acutely jealous. She could understand that her husband was worried, dissatisfied with himself, and ashamed, and when people are ashamed they hold aloof, above all from those nearest to them, and are unreserved with strangers; she could understand, also, that she had nothing to fear from Lubochka or from those women who were now drinking coffee indoors. But everything in general was terrible, incomprehensible, and it already seemed to Olga Mikhalovna that Pyotr Dmitrich only half belonged to her.

"He has no right to do it!" she muttered, trying to formulate her jealousy and her vexation with her husband. "He has no right at all. I will tell him so plainly!"

She made up her mind to find her husband at once and tell him all about it: it was disgusting, absolutely disgusting, that he was attractive to other women and sought their admiration as though it were some heavenly manna; it was unjust and dishonorable that he should give to others what belonged by right to his wife, that he should hide his soul and his conscience from his wife to reveal them to the first pretty face he came across. What harm had his wife done him? How was she to blame? Long ago she had been sickened by his lying: he was forever posing, flirting, saying what he did not think, and trying to seem different from what he was and what he ought to be. Why this falsity? Was it seemly in a decent man? If he lied he was demeaning himself and those to whom he lied, and slighting what he lied about. Could he not understand that if he swaggered and posed at the judicial table, or held forth at dinner on the prerogatives of Government, that he, simply to provoke her uncle, was showing thereby that he had not an ounce of respect for the Court, or himself, or any of the people who were listening and looking at him?

Coming out into the big avenue, Olga Mikhalovna assumed an expression of face as though she had just gone away to look after some domestic matter. In the verandah the gentlemen were drinking liqueur and eating strawberries: one of them, the Examining Magistrate—a stout, elderly man, a joker and wit—must have been telling some rather free anecdote, for, seeing their hostess, he suddenly clapped his hands over his fat lips, rolled his eyes, and sat down. Olga Mikhalovna did not like the local officials. She did not care for their clumsy, ceremonious wives, their scandal-mongering, their frequent visits, their flattery of her husband, whom they all hated. Now, when they were drinking, were replete with food and showed no signs of going away, she felt their presence an agonizing weariness; but not to appear impolite, she smiled cordially to the Magistrate, and shook her finger at him. She walked across the dining-room and drawing-room smiling, and looking as though she had gone to give some order and make some arrangement. "God grant no one stops me," she thought, but she forced herself to stop in the drawing-room to listen from politeness to a young man who was sitting at the piano playing: after standing for a minute, she cried, "Bravo, bravo, Monsieur Georges!" and clapping her hands twice, she went on.

She found her husband in his study. He was sitting at the table, thinking of something. His face looked stern, thoughtful, and guilty. This was not the same Pyotr Dmitrich who had been arguing at dinner and whom his guests knew, but a different man—wearied, feeling guilty and dissatisfied with himself, whom nobody knew but his wife. He must have come to the study to get cigarettes. Before him lay an open cigarette-case full of cigarettes, and one of his hands was in the table drawer; he had paused and sunk into thought as he was taking the cigarettes.

Olga Mikhalovna felt sorry for him. It was as clear as day that this man was harassed, could find no rest, and was perhaps struggling with himself. Olga Mikhalovna went up to the table in silence: wanting to show that she had forgotten the argument at dinner and was not cross, she shut the cigarette-case and put it in her husband's coat pocket.

"What should I say to him?" she wondered; "I shall say that lying is like a forest—the further one goes into it the more difficult it is to get out of it. I will say to him, 'You have been carried away by the false part you are playing; you have insulted people who were attached to you and have done you no harm. Go and apologize to them, laugh at yourself, and you will feel better. And if you want peace and solitude, let us go away together.' "

Meeting his wife's gaze, Pyotr Dmitrich's face immediately assumed the expression it had worn at dinner and in the garden—indifferent and slightly ironical. He yawned and got up.

"It's past five," he said, looking at his watch. "If our visitors are merciful and leave us at eleven, even then we have another six hours of it. It's a cheerful prospect, there's no denying!"

And whistling something, he walked slowly out of the study with his usual dignified gait. She could hear him with dignified firmness cross the dining-room, then the drawing-room, laugh with dignified assurance, and say to the young man who was playing, "Bravo! bravo!" Soon his footsteps died away: he must have gone out into the garden. And now not jealousy, not vexation, but real hatred of his footsteps, his insincere laugh and voice, took possession of Olga Mikhalovna. She went to the window and looked out into the garden. Pyotr Dmitrich was already walking along the avenue. Putting one hand in his pocket and snapping the fingers of the other, he walked with confident, swinging steps, throwing his head back a little, and looking as though he were very well satisfied with himself, with his dinner, with his digestion, and with nature. . . .

Two little schoolboys, the children of Madame Chizhevsky, who had only just arrived, made their appearance in the avenue, accompanied by their tutor, a student wearing a white tunic and very narrow trousers. When they reached Pyotr Dmitrich, the boys and the student stopped, and probably congratulated him on his name-day. With a graceful swing of his shoulders, he patted the children on their cheeks, and carelessly offered the student his hand without looking at him. The student must have praised the weather and compared it with the climate of Petersburg, for Pyotr Dmitrich said in a loud voice, in a tone as though he were not speaking to a guest, but to an usher of the court or a witness:

"What! It's cold in Petersburg? And here, my good sir, we have a salubrious atmosphere and the fruits of the earth in abundance. Eh? What?"

And thrusting one hand in his pocket and snapping the fingers of the other, he walked on. Till he had disappeared behind the nut bushes, Olga Mikhalovna watched the back of his head in perplexity. How had this man of thirty-four come by the dignified deportment of a general? How had he come by that impressive, elegant manner? Where had he got that vibration of authority in his voice? Where had he got these "what's," "to be sure's," and "my good sir's"?

Olga Mikhalovna remembered how in the first months of her marriage she had felt dreary at home alone and had driven into the town to the Circuit Court, at which Pyotr Dmitrich had sometimes presided in place of her godfather, Count Alexey Petrovich. In the presidential chair, wearing his uniform and a chain on his breast, he was completely changed. Stately gestures, a voice of thunder, "what," "to be sure," careless tones. . . . Everything, all that was ordinary and human, all that was individual and personal to himself that Olga Mikhalovna was accustomed to seeing in him at home, vanished in grandeur, and in the presidential chair there sat not Pyotr Dmitrich, but another man whom everyone called Mr. President.

This consciousness of power prevented him from sitting still in his place, and he seized every opportunity to ring his bell, to glance sternly at the public, to shout. . . . Where had he got his short-sight and his deafness when he suddenly began to see and hear with difficulty, and, frowning majestically, insisted on people speaking louder and coming closer to the table? From the height of his grandeur he could hardly distinguish faces or sounds, so that it seemed that if Olga Mikhalovna herself had gone up to him he would have shouted even to her, "Your name?" Peasant witnesses he addressed familiarly, he shouted at the public so that his voice could be heard even in the street, and behaved incredibly with the lawyers. If a lawyer had to speak to him, Pyotr Dmitrich, turning a little away from him, looked with half-closed eyes at the ceiling, meaning to signify thereby that the lawyer was utterly superfluous and that he was neither recognizing him nor listening to him; if a badly-dressed lawyer spoke, Pyotr Dmitrich pricked up his ears and looked the man up and down with a sarcastic, annihilating stare as though to say: "Queer sort of lawyers nowadays!"

"What do you mean by that?" he would interrupt.

If a would-be eloquent lawyer mispronounced a foreign word, saying, for instance, "factitious" instead of "fictitious," Pyotr Dmitrich brightened up at once and asked, "What? How? Factitious? What does that mean?" and then observed impressively: "Don't make use of words you do not understand." And the lawyer, finishing his speech, would walk away from the table, red and perspiring, while Pyotr Dmitrich, with a self-satisfied smile, would lean back in his chair triumphantly. In his manner with the lawyers he imitated Count Alexey Petrovich a little, but when the latter said, for instance, "Counsel for the defense, you keep quiet for a little!" it sounded paternally good-natured and natural, while the same words in Pyotr Dmitrich's mouth were rude and artificial.

II

There were sounds of applause. The young man had finished playing. Olga Mikhalovna remembered her guests and hurried into the drawing-room.

"I have so enjoyed your playing," she said, going up to the piano. "I have so enjoyed it. You have a wonderful talent! But don't you think our piano's out of tune?"

At that moment the two schoolboys walked into the room, accompanied by the student.

"My goodness! Mitya and Kolya," Olga Mikhalovna drawled joyfully, going to meet them: "How big they have grown! One would not know you! But where is your mamma?"

"I congratulate you on the name-day," the student began in a free-and-easy tone, "and I wish you all happiness. Ekaterina Andreyevna sends her congratulations and begs you to excuse her. She is not very well."

"How unkind of her! I have been expecting her all day. Is it long since you left Petersburg?" Olga Mikhalovna asked the student. "What kind of weather have you there now?" And without waiting for an answer, she looked cordially at the schoolboys and repeated:

"How tall they have grown! It is not long since they used to come with their nurse, and they are at school already! The old grow older while the young grow up. . . . Have you had dinner?"

"Oh, please don't trouble!" said the student.

"Why, you have not had dinner?"

"For goodness' sake, don't trouble!"

"But I suppose you are hungry?" Olga Mikhalovna said it in a harsh, rude voice, with impatience and vexation—it escaped her unawares, but at once she coughed, smiled, and flushed crimson. "How tall they have grown!" she said softly.

"Please don't trouble!" the student said once more.

The student begged her not to trouble; the boys said nothing; obviously all three of them were hungry. Olga Mikhalovna took them into the dining-room and told Vassily to lay the table.

"How unkind of your mamma!" she said as she made them sit down.

"She has quite forgotten me. Unkind, unkind, unkind . . . you must tell her so. What are you studying?" she asked the student.

"Medicine."

"Well, I have a weakness for doctors, only fancy. I am very sorry my husband is not a doctor. What courage anyone must have to perform an operation or dissect a corpse, for instance! Horrible! Aren't you frightened? I believe I should die of terror! Of course, you drink vodka?"

"Please don't trouble."

"After your journey you must have something to drink. Though I am a woman, even I drink sometimes. And Mitya and Kolya will drink Malaga. It's not a strong wine; you need not be afraid of it. What fine fellows they are, really! They'll be thinking of getting married next."

Olga Mikhalovna talked without ceasing; she knew by experience that when she had guests to entertain it was far easier and more comfortable to talk than to listen. When you talk there is no need to strain your attention to think of answers to questions, and to change your expression of face. But unawares she asked the student a serious question; the student began a lengthy speech and she was forced to listen. The student knew that she had once been at the University, and so tried to seem a serious person as he talked to her.

"What subject are you studying?" she asked, forgetting that she had already put that question to him.

"Medicine."

Olga Mikhalovna now remembered that she had been away from the ladies for a long while.

"Yes? Then I suppose you are going to be a doctor?" she said, getting up. "That's splendid. I am sorry I did not go in for medicine myself. So you will finish your dinner here, gentlemen, and then come into the garden. I will introduce you to the young ladies."

She went out and glanced at her watch: it was five minutes to six. And she wondered that the time had gone so slowly, and thought with horror that there were six more hours before midnight, when the party would break up. How could she get through those six hours? What phrases could she utter? How should she behave to her husband?

There was not a soul in the drawing-room or on the verandah. All the guests were sauntering about the garden.

"I shall have to suggest a walk in the birchwood before tea, or else a row in the boats," thought Olga Mikhalovna, hurrying to the croquet ground, from which came the sounds of voices and laughter.

"And sit the old people down to *vint*. . . ." She met Grigory the footman coming from the croquet ground with empty bottles.

"Where are the ladies?" she asked.

"Among the raspberry-bushes. The master's there, too."

"Oh, good heavens!" someone on the croquet lawn shouted with exasperation. "I have told you a thousand times over! To know the Bulgarians you must see them! You can't judge from the papers!"

Either because of the outburst or for some other reason, Olga Mikhalovna was suddenly aware of a terrible weakness all over, especially in her legs and in her shoulders. She felt she could not bear to speak, to listen, or to move.

"Grigory," she said faintly and with an effort, "when you have to serve tea or anything, please don't appeal to me, don't ask me anything, don't speak of anything. . . . Do it all yourself, and . . . and don't make a noise with your feet, I entreat you. . . . I can't, because . . ."

Without finishing, she walked on towards the croquet lawn, but on the way she thought of the ladies, and turned towards the raspberry-bushes. The sky, the air, and the trees looked gloomy again and threatened rain; it was hot and stifling. An immense flock of crows, foreseeing a storm, flew cawing over the garden. The paths were more overgrown, darker, and narrower as they got nearer the kitchen garden. In one of them, buried in a thick tangle of wild pear, crab-apple, sorrel, young oaks, and hopbine, clouds of tiny black flies swarmed round Olga Mikhalovna. She covered her face with her hands and began forcing herself to think of the little creature . . . . There floated through her imagination the figures of Grigory, Mitya, Kolya, the faces of the peasants who had come in the morning to present their congratulations.

She heard footsteps, and she opened her eyes. Uncle Nikolai Nikolaich was coming rapidly towards her.

"It's you, dear? I am very glad . . ." he began, breathless. "A couple of words. . . ." He mopped with his handkerchief his red shaven chin, then suddenly stepped back a pace, flung up his hands, and opened his eyes wide. "My dear girl, how long is this going on?" he said rapidly, spluttering. "I ask you: is there no limit to it? I say nothing of the demoralizing effect of his martinet views on all around him, of the way he insults all that is sacred and best in me and in every honest thinking man—I will say nothing about that, but he might at least behave decently! Why, he shouts, he bellows, gives himself airs, poses as a sort of Bonaparte, does not let one say a word. . . . I don't know what the devil's the matter with him! These lordly gestures, this condescending tone; and laughing like a general! Who is he, allow me to ask you? I ask you, who is he? The husband of his wife, with a few paltry acres and the rank of a titular who has had the luck to marry an heiress! An upstart and a *junker*, like so many others! A type out of Shchedrin! Upon my word, it's either that he's suffering from megalomania, or that old rat in his dotage, Count Alexey Petrovich, is right when he says that children and young people are a long time growing up nowadays, and go on playing they are cabmen and generals till they are forty!"

"That's true, that's true," Olga Mikhalovna assented. "Let me pass."

"Now just consider: what is it leading to?" her uncle went on, barring her way. "How will this playing at being a general and a Conservative end? Already he has got into trouble! Yes, to stand his trial! I am very glad of it! That's what his noise and shouting has brought him to—to stand in the prisoner's dock. And it's not as though it were the Circuit Court or something: it's the Central Court! Nothing worse could be imagined, I think! And then he has quarreled with everyone! He is celebrating his name-day, and look, Vostryakov's not here, nor Yakhontov, nor Vladimirov, nor Shevud, nor the Count. . . . There is no one, I imagine, more Conservative than Count Alexey Petrovich, yet even he has not come. And he never will come again. He won't come, you will see!"

"My God! but what has it to do with me?" asked Olga Mikhalovna.

"What has it to do with you? Why, you are his wife! You are clever, you have had a university education, and it was in your power to make him an honest worker!"

"At the lectures I went to they did not teach us how to influence tiresome people. It seems as though I should have to apologize to all of you for having been at the University," said Olga Mikhalovna sharply. "Listen, uncle. If people played the same scales over and over again the whole day long in your hearing, you wouldn't be able to sit still and listen, but would run away. I hear the same thing over again for days together all the year round. You must have pity on me at last."

Her uncle pulled a very long face, then looked at her searchingly and twisted his lips into a mocking smile.

"So that's how it is," he piped in a voice like an old woman's. "I beg your pardon!" he said, and made a ceremonious bow. "If you have fallen under his influence yourself, and have abandoned your convictions, you should have said so before. I beg your pardon!"

"Yes, I have abandoned my convictions," she cried. "There; make the most of it!"

"I beg your pardon!"

Her uncle for the last time made her a ceremonious bow, a little on one side, and, shrinking into himself, made a scrape with his foot and walked back.

"Idiot!" thought Olga Mikhalovna. "I hope he will go home."

She found the ladies and the young people among the raspberries in the kitchen garden. Some were eating raspberries; others, tired of eating raspberries, were strolling about the strawberry beds or foraging among the sugar-peas. A little on one side of the raspberry bed, near a branching apple tree propped up by posts which had been pulled out of an old fence, Pyotr Dmitrich was mowing the grass. His hair was falling over his forehead, his cravat was untied. His watch-chain was hanging loose. Every step and every swing of the scythe showed skill and the possession of immense physical strength. Near him were standing Lubochka and the daughters of a neighbor, Colonel Bukryeev—two anaemic and unhealthily stout, fair girls, Natalya and Valentina, or, as they were always called, Nata and Vata, both wearing white frocks and strikingly like each other. Pyotr Dmitrich was teaching them to mow.

"It's very simple," he said. "You have only to know how to hold the scythe and not to get too hot over it—that is, not to use more force than is necessary! Like this. . . . Wouldn't you like to try?" he said, offering the scythe to Lubochka. "Come!"

Lubochka took the scythe clumsily, blushed crimson, and laughed.

"Don't be afraid, Lubov Alexandrovna!" cried Olga Mikhalovna, loud enough for all the ladies to hear that she was with them. "Don't be afraid! You must learn! If you marry a Tolstoyan he will make you mow."

Lubochka raised the scythe, but began laughing again, and, helpless with laughter, let go of it at once. She was ashamed and pleased at being talked to as though grown up. Nata, with a cold, serious face, with no trace of smiling or shyness, took the scythe, swung it, and caught it in the grass; Vata, also without a smile, as cold and serious as her sister, took the scythe, and silently thrust it into the earth. Having done this, the two sisters linked arms and walked in silence to the raspberries.

Pyotr Dmitrich laughed and played about like a boy, and this childish, frolicsome mood in which he became exceedingly good-natured suited him far better than any other. Olga Mikhalovna loved him when he was like that. But his boyishness did not usually last long. It did not this time; after playing with the scythe, he for some reason thought it necessary to take a serious tone about it.

"When I am mowing, I feel, do you know, healthier and more normal," he said. "If I were forced to confine myself to an intellectual life I believe I should go out of my mind. I feel that I was not born to be a man of culture! I ought to mow, plough, sow, drive out the horses."

And Pyotr Dmitrich began a conversation with the ladies about the advantages of physical labor, about culture, and then about the pernicious effects of money, of property. Listening to her husband, Olga Mikhalovna, for some reason, thought of her dowry.

"And the time will come, I suppose," she thought, "when he will not forgive me for being richer than he. He is proud and vain. Maybe he will hate me because he owes so much to me."

She stopped near Colonel Bukryeev, who was eating raspberries and also taking part in the conversation.

"Come," he said, making room for Olga Mikhalovna and Pyotr Dmitrich. "The ripest are here. . . . And so, according to Proudhon," he went on, raising his voice, "property is robbery. But I must confess I don't believe in Proudhon, and don't consider him a philosopher. The French are not authorities, to my thinking—God bless them!"

"Well, as for Proudhons and Buckles and the rest of them, I am weak in that department," said Pyotr Dmitrich. "For philosophy you must apply to my wife. She has been at University lectures and knows all your Schopenhauers and Proudhons by heart. . . ."

Olga Mikhalovna felt bored again. She walked again along a little path by apple and pear trees, and looked again as though she was on some very important errand. She reached the gardener's cottage. In the doorway the gardener's wife, Varvara, was sitting together with her four little children with big shaven heads. Varvara, too, was with child and expecting to be confined on Elijah's Day. After greeting her, Olga Mikhalovna looked at her and the children in silence and asked:

"Well, how do you feel?"

"Oh, all right. . . ."

A silence followed. The two women seemed to understand each other without words.

"It's dreadful having one's first baby," said Olga Mikhalovna after a moment's thought. "I keep feeling as though I shall not get through it, as though I shall die."

"I fancied that, too, but here I am alive. One has all sorts of fancies."

Varvara, who was just going to have her fifth, looked down a little on her mistress from the height of her experience and spoke in a rather didactic tone, and Olga Mikhalovna could not help feeling her authority; she would have liked to have talked of her fears, of the child, of her sensations, but she was afraid it might strike Varvara as naïve and trivial. And she waited in silence for Varvara to say something herself.

"Olya, we are going indoors," Pyotr Dmitrich called from the raspberries.

Olga Mikhalovna liked being silent, waiting and watching Varvara. She would have been ready to stay like that till night without speaking or having any duty to perform. But she had to go. She had hardly left the cottage when Lubochka, Nata, and Vata came running to meet her. The sisters stopped short abruptly a couple of yards away; Lubochka ran right up to her and flung herself on her neck.

"You dear, darling, precious," she said, kissing her face and her neck. "Let us go and have tea on the island!"

"On the island, on the island!" said the precisely similar Nata and Vata, both at once, without a smile.

"But it's going to rain, my dears."

"It's not, it's not," cried Lubochka with a woebegone face. "They've all agreed to go. Dear! darling!"

"They are all getting ready to have tea on the island," said Pyotr Dmitrich, coming up. "See to arranging things. . . . We will all go in the boats, and the samovars and all the rest of it must be sent in the carriage with the servants."

He walked beside his wife and gave her his arm. Olga Mikhalovna had a desire to say something disagreeable to her husband, something biting, even about her dowry perhaps—the crueller the better, she felt. She thought a little, and said:

"Why is it Count Alexey Petrovich hasn't come? What a pity!"

"I am very glad he hasn't come," said Pyotr Dmitrich, lying. "I'm sick to death of that old lunatic."

"But yet before dinner you were expecting him so eagerly!"

III

Half an hour later all the guests were crowding on the bank near the piling to which the boats were fastened. They were all talking and laughing, and were in such excitement and commotion that they could hardly get into the boats. Three boats were crammed with passengers, while two stood empty. The keys for unfastening these two boats had been somehow mislaid, and messengers were continually running from the river to the house to look for them. Some said Grigory had the keys, others that the bailiff had them, while others suggested sending for a blacksmith and breaking the padlocks. And all talked at once, interrupting and shouting one another down. Pyotr Dmitrich paced impatiently to and fro on the bank, shouting:

"What the devil's the meaning of it! The keys ought always to be lying in the hall window! Who has dared to take them away? The bailiff can get a boat of his own if he wants one!"

At last the keys were found. Then it appeared that two oars were missing. Again there was a great hullabaloo. Pyotr Dmitrich, who was weary of pacing about the bank, jumped into a long, narrow boat hollowed out of the trunk of a poplar, and, lurching from side to side and almost falling into the water, pushed off from the bank. The other boats followed him one after another, amid loud laughter and the shrieks of the young ladies.

The white cloudy sky, the trees on the riverside, the boats with the people in them, and the oars, were reflected in the water as in a mirror; under the boats, far away below in the bottomless depths, was a second sky with the birds flying across it. The bank on which the house and gardens stood was high, steep, and covered with trees; on the other, which was sloping, stretched broad, green water-meadows with sheets of water glistening in them. The boats had floated a hundred yards when, behind the mournfully drooping willows on the sloping banks, huts and a herd of cows came into sight; they began to hear songs, drunken shouts, and the strains of a concertina.

Here and there on the river fishing-boats were scattered about, setting their nets for the night. In one of these boats was the festive party, playing on home-made violins and violoncellos.

Olga Mikhalovna was sitting at the rudder; she was smiling affably and talking a great deal to entertain her visitors, while she glanced stealthily at her husband. He was ahead of them all, standing up punting with one oar. The light, sharp-nosed canoe, which all the guests called the "death trap"—while Pyotr Dmitrich, for some reason, called it *Penderaklia*—flew along quickly; it had a brisk, crafty expression, as though it hated its heavy occupant and was looking out for a favorable moment to glide away from under his feet. Olga Mikhalovna kept looking at her husband, and she loathed his good looks which attracted everyone, the back of his head, his attitude, his familiar manner with women; she hated all the women sitting in the boat with her, was jealous, and at the same time was trembling every minute in terror that the frail craft would upset and cause an accident.

"Take care, Pyotr!" she cried, while her heart fluttered with terror. "Sit down! We believe in your courage without all that!"

She was worried, too, by the people who were in the boat with her. They were all ordinary good sort of people like thousands of others, but now each one of them struck her as exceptional and evil. In each one of them she saw nothing but falsity. "That young man," she thought, "rowing, in gold-rimmed spectacles, with chestnut hair and a nice-looking beard: he is a mamma's darling, rich, and well-fed, and always fortunate, and everyone considers him an honorable, free-thinking, advanced man. It's not a year since he left the University and came to live in the district, but he already talks of himself as 'we active members of the Zemstvo.' But in another year he will be bored like so many others and go off to Petersburg, and to justify running away, will tell everyone that the Zemstvos are good-for-nothing, and that he has been deceived in them. While from the other boat his young wife keeps her eyes fixed on him, and believes that he is 'an active member of the Zemstvo,' just as in a year she will believe that the Zemstvo is good-for-nothing. And that stout, carefully shaven gentleman in the straw hat with the broad ribbon, with an expensive cigar in his mouth: he is fond of saying, 'It is time to put away dreams and set to work!' He has Yorkshire pigs, Butler's hives, rape-seed, pine-apples, a dairy, a cheese factory, Italian bookkeeping by double entry; but every summer he sells his timber and mortgages part of his land to spend the autumn with his mistress in the Crimea. And there's Uncle Nikolai Nikolaich, who has quarreled with Pyotr Dmitrich, and yet for some reason does not go home."

Olga Mikhalovna looked at the other boats, and there, too, she saw only uninteresting, queer creatures, affected or stupid people. She thought of all the people she knew in the district, and could not remember one person of whom one could say or think anything good. They all seemed to her mediocre, insipid, unintelligent, narrow, false, heartless; they all said what they did not think, and did what they did not want to. Dreariness and despair were stifling her; she longed to leave off smiling, to leap up and cry out, "I am sick of you," and then jump out and swim to the bank.

"I say, let's take Pyotr Dmitrich in tow!" someone shouted.

"In tow, in tow!" the others chimed in. "Olga Mikhalovna, take your husband in tow."

To take him in tow, Olga Mikhalovna, who was steering, had to seize the right moment and to catch hold of his boat by the chain at the beak. When she bent over to the chain Pyotr Dmitrich frowned and looked at her in alarm.

"I hope you won't catch cold," he said.

"If you are uneasy about me and the child, why do you torment me?" thought Olga Mikhalovna.

Pyotr Dmitrich acknowledged himself vanquished, and, not caring to be towed, jumped from the *Penderaklia* into the boat which was overfull already, and jumped so carelessly that the boat lurched violently, and everyone cried out in terror.

"He did that to please the ladies," thought Olga Mikhalovna; "he knows it's charming." Her hands and feet began trembling, as she supposed, from boredom, vexation from the strain of smiling, and the discomfort she felt all over her body. And to conceal this trembling from her guests, she tried to talk more loudly, to laugh, to move.

"If I suddenly begin to cry," she thought, "I shall say I have toothache. . . ."

But at last the boats reached the "Island of Good Hope," as they called the peninsula formed by a bend in the river at an acute angle, covered with a grove of old birch-trees, oaks, willows, and poplars. The tables were already laid under the trees; the samovars were smoking, and Vassily and Grigory, in their swallow-tails and white knitted gloves, were already busy with the tea-things. On the other bank, opposite the "Island of Good Hope," there stood the carriages which had come with the provisions. The baskets and parcels of provisions were carried across to the island in a little boat like the *Penderaklia*. The footmen, the coachmen, and even the peasant who was sitting in the boat had the solemn expression befitting a name-day such as one only sees in children and servants.

While Olga Mikhalovna was making the tea and pouring out the first glasses, the visitors were busy with the liqueurs and sweet things. Then there was the general commotion usual at picnics over drinking tea, very wearisome and exhausting for the hostess. Grigory and Vassily had hardly had time to take the glasses round before hands were being stretched out to Olga Mikhalovna with empty glasses. One asked for no sugar, another wanted it stronger, another weak, a fourth declined another glass. And all this Olga Mikhalovna had to remember, and then to call, "Ivan Petrovich, is it without sugar for you?" or, "Gentlemen, which of you wanted it weak?" But the guest who had asked for weak tea, or no sugar, had by now forgotten it, and, absorbed in agreeable conversation, took the first glass that came. Depressed-looking figures wandered like shadows at a little distance from the table, pretending to look for mushrooms in the grass, or reading the labels on the boxes—these were those for whom there were not glasses enough. "Have you had tea?" Olga Mikhalovna kept asking, and the guest so addressed begged her not to trouble, and said, "I will wait," though it would have suited her better for the visitors not to wait but to make haste.

Some, absorbed in conversation, drank their tea slowly, keeping their glasses for half an hour; others, especially some who had drunk a good deal at dinner, would not leave the table, and kept on drinking glass after glass, so that Olga Mikhalovna scarcely had time to fill them. One jocular young man sipped his tea through a lump of sugar, and kept saying, "Sinful man that I am, I love to indulge myself with the Chinese herb." He kept asking with a heavy sigh: "Another tiny dish of tea more, if you please." He drank a great deal, nibbled his sugar, and thought it all very amusing and original, and imagined that he was doing a clever imitation of a Russian merchant. None of them understood that these trifles were agonizing to their hostess, and, indeed, it was hard to understand it, as Olga Mikhalovna went on all the time smiling affably and talking nonsense.

But she felt ill. . . . She was irritated by the crowd of people, the laughter, the questions, the jocular young man, the footmen harassed and run off their legs, the children who hung round the table; she was irritated at Vata's being like Nata, at Kolya's being like Mitya, so that one could not tell which of them had had tea and which of them had not. She felt that her smile of forced affability was passing into an expression of anger, and she felt every minute as though she would burst into tears.

"Rain, my friends," cried someone.

Everyone looked at the sky.

"Yes, it really is rain . . ." Pyotr Dmitrich assented, and wiped his cheek.

Only a few drops were falling from the sky—the real rain had not begun yet; but the company abandoned their tea and made haste to get off. At first they all wanted to drive home in the carriages, but changed their minds and made for the boats. On the pretext that she had to hasten home to give directions about the supper, Olga Mikhalovna asked to be excused for leaving the others, and went home in the carriage.

When she got into the carriage, she first of all let her face rest from smiling. With an angry face she drove through the village, and with an angry face acknowledged the bows of the peasants she met. When she got home, she went to the bedroom by the back way and lay down on her husband's bed.

"Merciful God!" she whispered. "What is all this hard labor for? Why do all these people hustle each other here and pretend that they are enjoying themselves? Why do I smile and lie? I don't understand it."

She heard steps and voices. The visitors had come back.

"Let them come," thought Olga Mikhalovna; "I shall lie a little longer."

But a maid-servant came and said:

"Marya Grigoryevna is going, madam."

Olga Mikhalovna jumped up, tidied her hair, and hurried out of the room.

"Marya Grigoryevna, what is the meaning of this?" she began in an injured voice, going to meet Marya Grigoryevna. "Why are you in such a hurry?"

"I can't help it, darling! I've stayed too long as it is; my children are expecting me home."

"It's too bad of you! Why didn't you bring your children with you?"

"If you will let me, dear, I will bring them on some ordinary day, but today . . ."

"Oh, please do," Olga Mikhalovna interrupted; "I shall be delighted! Your children are so sweet! Kiss them all for me. . . . But, really, I am offended with you! I don't understand why you are in such a hurry!"

"I really must, I really must. . . . Goodbye, dear. Take care of yourself. In your condition, you know . . ."

And the ladies kissed each other. After seeing the departing guest to her carriage, Olga Mikhalovna went in to the ladies in the drawing-room. There the lamps were already lighted and the gentlemen were sitting down to cards.

IV

The party broke up after supper about a quarter past twelve. Seeing her visitors off, Olga Mikhalovna stood at the door and said:

"You really ought to take a shawl! It's turning a little chilly. Please God, you don't catch cold!"

"Don't trouble, Olga Mikhalovna," the ladies answered as they got into the carriage. "Well, goodbye. Mind now, we are expecting you; don't play us false!"

"Wo-o-o!" the coachman checked the horses.

"Ready, Denis! Goodbye, Olga Mikhalovna!"

"Kiss the children for me!"

The carriage started and immediately disappeared into the darkness. In the red circle of light cast by the lamp in the road, a fresh pair or trio of impatient horses, and the silhouette of a coachman with his hands held out stiffly before him, would come into view. Again there began kisses, reproaches, and entreaties to come again or to take a shawl. Pyotr Dmitrich kept running out and helping the ladies into their carriages.

"You go now by Efremovshchina," he directed the coachman; "it's nearer through Mankino, but the road is worse that way. You might have an upset. . . . Goodbye, my charmer. *Mille* compliments to your artist!"

"Goodbye, Olga Mikhalovna, darling! Go indoors, or you will catch cold! It's damp!"

"Wo-o-o! You rascal!"

"What horses have you got here?" Pyotr Dmitrich asked.

"They were bought from Khaidorov, in Lent," answered the coachman.

"Capital horses. . . ."

And Pyotr Dmitrich patted the trace horse on the haunch.

"Well, you can start! God give you good luck!"

The last visitor was gone at last; the red circle on the road quivered, moved aside, contracted, and went out, as Vassily carried away the lamp from the entrance. On previous occasions when they had seen off their visitors, Pyotr Dmitrich and Olga Mikhalovna had begun dancing about the drawing-room, facing each other, clapping their hands, and singing: "They've gone! They've gone!" But now Olga Mikhalovna was not equal to that. She went to her bedroom, undressed, and got into bed.

She fancied she would fall asleep at once and sleep soundly. Her legs and her shoulders ached painfully, her head was heavy from the strain of talking, and she was conscious, as before, of discomfort all over her body. Covering her head over, she lay still for three or four minutes, then peeped out from under the bed-clothes at the lamp before the ikon, listened to the silence, and smiled.

"It's nice, it's nice," she whispered, curling up her legs, which felt as if they had grown longer from so much walking. "Sleep, sleep. . . ."

Her legs would not get into a comfortable position; she felt uneasy all over, and she turned on the other side. A big fly blew buzzing about the bedroom and thumped against the ceiling. She could hear, too, Grigory and Vassily stepping cautiously about the drawing-room, putting the chairs back in their places; it seemed to Olga Mikhalovna that she could not go to sleep, nor be comfortable till those sounds were hushed. And again she turned over on the other side impatiently.

She heard her husband's voice in the drawing-room. Someone must be staying the night, as Pyotr Dmitrich was addressing someone and speaking loudly:

"I don't say that Count Alexey Petrovich is an impostor. But he can't help seeming to be one, because all of you gentlemen attempt to see in him something different from what he really is. His craziness is looked upon as originality, his familiar manners as good-nature, and his complete absence of opinions as Conservatism. Even granted that he is a Conservative of the stamp of '84, what after all is Conservatism?"

Pyotr Dmitrich, angry with Count Alexey Petrovich, his visitors, and himself, was relieving his heart. He abused both the Count and his visitors, and in his vexation with himself was ready to speak out and to hold forth upon anything. After seeing his guest to his room, he walked up and down the drawing-room, walked through the dining-room, down the corridor, then into his study, then again went into the drawing-room, and came into the bedroom. Olga Mikhalovna was lying on her back, with the bed-clothes only to her waist (by now she felt hot), and with an angry face, watched the fly that was thumping against the ceiling.

"Is someone staying the night?" she asked.

"Yegorov."

Pyotr Dmitrich undressed and got into his bed.

Without speaking, he lighted a cigarette, and he, too, fell to watching the fly. There was an uneasy and forbidding look in his eyes. Olga Mikhalovna looked at his handsome profile for five minutes in silence. It seemed to her for some reason that if her husband were suddenly to turn facing her, and to say, "Olga, I am unhappy," she would cry or laugh, and she would be at ease. She fancied that her legs were aching and her body was uncomfortable all over because of the strain on her feelings.

"Pyotr, what are you thinking of?" she said.

"Oh, nothing . . ." her husband answered.

"You have taken to having secrets from me of late: that's not right."

"Why is it not right?" answered Pyotr Dmitrich drily and not at once. "We all have our personal life, every one of us, and we are bound to have our secrets."

"Personal life, our secrets . . . that's all words! Understand you are wounding me!" said Olga Mikhalovna, sitting up in bed. "If you have a load on your heart, why do you hide it from me? And why do you find it more suitable to open your heart to women who are nothing to you, instead of to your wife? I overheard your outpourings to Lubochka by the bee-house today."

"Well, I congratulate you. I am glad you did overhear it."

This meant "Leave me alone and let me think." Olga Mikhalovna was indignant. Vexation, hatred, and wrath, which had been accumulating within her during the whole day, suddenly boiled over; she wanted at once to speak out, to hurt her husband without putting it off till tomorrow, to wound him, to punish him. . . . Making an effort to control herself and not to scream, she said:

"Let me tell you, then, that it's all loathsome, loathsome, loathsome! I've been hating you all day; you see what you've done."

Pyotr Dmitrich, too, got up and sat on the bed.

"It's loathsome, loathsome, loathsome," Olga Mikhalovna went on, beginning to tremble all over. "There's no need to congratulate me; you had better congratulate yourself! It's a shame, a disgrace. You have wrapped yourself in lies till you are ashamed to be alone in the room with your wife! You are a deceitful man! I see through you and understand every step you take!"

"Olya, I wish you would please warn me when you are out of humor. Then I will sleep in the study."

Saying this, Pyotr Dmitrich picked up his pillow and walked out of the bedroom. Olga Mikhalovna had not foreseen this. For some minutes she remained silent with her mouth open, trembling all over and looking at the door by which her husband had gone out, and trying to understand what it meant. Was this one of the devices to which deceitful people have recourse when they are in the wrong, or was it a deliberate insult aimed at her pride? How was she to take it? Olga Mikhalovna remembered her cousin, a lively young officer, who often used to tell her, laughing, that when "his spouse nagged at him" at night, he usually picked up his pillow and went whistling to spend the night in his study, leaving his wife in a foolish and ridiculous position. This officer was married to a rich, capricious, and foolish woman whom he did not respect but simply put up with.

Olga Mikhalovna jumped out of bed. To her mind there was only one thing left for her to do now; to dress with all possible haste and to leave the house forever. The house was her own, but so much the worse for Pyotr Dmitrich. Without pausing to consider whether this was necessary or not, she went quickly to the study to inform her husband of her intention ("Feminine logic!" flashed through her mind), and to say something wounding and sarcastic at parting. . . .

Pyotr Dmitrich was lying on the sofa and pretending to read a newspaper. There was a candle burning on a chair near him. His face could not be seen behind the newspaper.

"Be so kind as to tell me what this means? I am asking you."

"Be so kind . . ." Pyotr Dmitrich mimicked her, not showing his face. "It's sickening, Olga! Upon my honor, I am exhausted and not up to it. . . . Let us do our quarrelling tomorrow."

"No, I understand you perfectly!" Olga Mikhalovna went on. "You hate me! Yes, yes! You hate me because I am richer than you! You will never forgive me for that, and will always be lying to me!" ("Feminine logic!" flashed through her mind again.) "You are laughing at me now. . . . I am convinced, in fact, that you only married me in order to have property qualifications and those wretched horses. . . . Oh, I am miserable!"

Pyotr Dmitrich dropped the newspaper and got up. The unexpected insult overwhelmed him. With a childishly helpless

smile he looked desperately at his wife, and holding out his hands
to her as though to ward off blows, he said imploringly:

"Olya!"

And expecting her to say something else awful, he leaned back
in his chair, and his huge figure seemed as helplessly childish as his
smile.

"Olya, how could you say it?" he whispered.

Olga Mikhalovna came to herself. She was suddenly aware of her
passionate love for this man, remembered that he was her husband,
Pyotr Dmitrich, without whom she could not live for a day, and
who loved her passionately, too. She burst into loud sobs that
sounded strange and unlike her, and ran back to her bedroom.

She fell on the bed, and short hysterical sobs, choking her and
making her arms and legs twitch, filled the bedroom. Remembering
there was a visitor sleeping three or four rooms away, she buried
her head under the pillow to stifle her sobs, but the pillow rolled
on to the floor, and she almost fell on the floor herself when she
stooped to pick it up. She pulled the quilt up to her face, but her
hands would not obey her, but tore convulsively at everything she
clutched.

She thought that everything was lost, that the falsehood she had
told to wound her husband had shattered her life into fragments.
Her husband would not forgive her. The insult she had hurled at
him was not one that could be effaced by any caresses, by any
vows. . . . How could she convince her husband that she did not
believe what she had said?

"It's all over, it's all over!" she cried, not noticing that the pillow
had slipped on to the floor again. "For God's sake, for God's sake!"

Probably roused by her cries, the guest and the servants were
now awake; next day all the neighborhood would know that she
had been in hysterics and would blame Pyotr Dmitrich. She made
an effort to restrain herself, but her sobs grew louder and louder
every minute.

"For God's sake," she cried in a voice not like her own, and not
knowing why she cried it. "For God's sake!"

She felt as though the bed were heaving under her and her feet
were entangled in the bed-clothes. Pyotr Dmitrich, in his dressing-
gown, with a candle in his hand, came into the bedroom.

"Olya, hush!" he said.

She raised herself, and kneeling up in bed, screwing up her eyes
at the light, articulated through her sobs:

"Understand . . . understand! . . ."

She wanted to tell him that she was tired to death by the party, by his falsity, by her own falsity, that it had all worked together, but she could only articulate:

"Understand . . . understand!"

"Come, drink!" he said, handing her some water.

She took the glass obediently and began drinking, but the water splashed over and was spilt on her arms, her throat and knees.

"I must look horribly unseemly," she thought.

Pyotr Dmitrich put her back in bed without a word, and covered her with the quilt, then he took the candle and went out.

"For God's sake!" Olga Mikhalovna cried again. "Pyotr, understand, understand!"

Suddenly something gripped her in the lower part of her body and back with such violence that her wailing was cut short, and she bit the pillow from the pain. But the pain let her go again at once, and she began sobbing again.

The maid came in, and arranging the quilt over her, asked in alarm:

"Mistress, darling, what is the matter?"

"Go out of the room," said Pyotr Dmitrich sternly, going up to the bed.

"Understand . . . understand! . . ." Olga Mikhalovna began.

"Olya, I entreat you, calm yourself," he said. "I did not mean to hurt you. I would not have gone out of the room if I had known it would have hurt you so much; I simply felt depressed. I tell you, on my honor . . ."

"Understand! . . . You were lying, I was lying. . . ."

"I understand. . . . Come, come, that's enough! I understand," said Pyotr Dmitrich tenderly, sitting down on her bed. "You said that in anger; I quite understand. I swear to God I love you beyond anything on earth, and when I married you I never once thought of your being rich. I loved you immensely, and that's all . . . I assure you. I have never been in want of money or felt the value of it, and so I cannot feel the difference between your fortune and mine. It always seemed to me we were equally well off. And that I have been deceitful in little things, that . . . of course, is true. My life has hitherto been arranged in such a frivolous way that it has somehow been impossible to get on without paltry lying. It weighs on me, too, now. . . . Let us leave off talking about it, for goodness' sake!"

Olga Mikhalovna again felt in acute pain, and clutched her husband by the sleeve.

"I am in pain, in pain, in pain . . ." she said rapidly. "Oh, what pain!"

"Damnation take those visitors!" muttered Pyotr Dmitrich, getting up. "You ought not to have gone to the island today!" he cried. "What an idiot I was not to prevent you! Oh, my God!"

He scratched his head in vexation, and, with a wave of his hand, walked out of the room.

Then he came into the room several times, sat down on the bed beside her, and talked a great deal, sometimes tenderly, sometimes angrily, but she hardly heard him. Her sobs were continually interrupted by fearful attacks of pain, and each time the pain was more acute and prolonged. At first she held her breath and bit the pillow during the pain, but then she began screaming on an unseemly piercing note.

Once seeing her husband near her, she remembered that she had insulted him, and without pausing to think whether it were really Pyotr Dmitrich or whether she were in delirium, clutched his hand in both hers and began kissing it.

"You were lying, I was lying . . ." she began justifying herself. "Understand, understand. . . . They have exhausted me, driven me out of all patience."

"Olya, we are not alone," said Pyotr Dmitrich.

Olga Mikhalovna raised her head and saw Varvara, who was kneeling by the chest of drawers and pulling out the bottom drawer. The top drawers were already open. Then Varvara got up, red from the strained position, and with a cold, solemn face began trying to unlock a box.

"Marya, I can't unlock it!" she said in a whisper. "You unlock it, won't you?"

Marya, the maid, was digging a candle end out of the candlestick with a pair of scissors, so as to put in a new candle; she went up to Varvara and helped her to unlock the box.

"There should be nothing locked . . ." whispered Varvara. "Unlock this basket, too, my good girl. Master," she said, "you should send to Father Mikhail to unlock the holy gates! You must!"

"Do what you like," said Pyotr Dmitrich, breathing hard, "only, for God's sake, make haste and fetch the doctor or the midwife! Has Vassily gone? Send someone else. Send your husband!"

"It's the birth," Olga Mikhalovna thought. "Varvara," she moaned, "but he won't be born alive!"

"It's all right, it's all right, mistress," whispered Varvara.

"Please God, he will be alive! he will be alive!"

When Olga Mikhalovna came to herself again after a pain she was no longer sobbing nor tossing from side to side, but moaning. She could not refrain from moaning even in the intervals between the pains.

The candles were still burning, but the morning light was coming through the blinds. It was probably about five o'clock in the morning. At the round table there was sitting some unknown woman with a very discreet air, wearing a white apron. From her whole appearance it was evident she had been sitting there a long time. Olga Mikhalovna guessed that she was the midwife.

"Will it soon be over?" she asked, and in her voice she heard a peculiar and unfamiliar note which had never been there before. "I must be dying in childbirth," she thought.

Pyotr Dmitrich came cautiously into the bedroom, dressed for the day, and stood at the window with his back to his wife. He lifted the blind and looked out of window.

"What rain!" he said.

"What time is it?" asked Olga Mikhalovna, in order to hear the unfamiliar note in her voice again.

"A quarter to six," answered the midwife.

"And what if I really am dying?" thought Olga Mikhalovna, looking at her husband's head and the window-panes on which the rain was beating. "How will he live without me? With whom will he have tea and dinner, talk in the evenings, sleep?"

And he seemed to her like a forlorn child; she felt sorry for him and wanted to say something nice, caressing, and consolatory. She remembered how in the spring he had meant to buy himself some hounds, and she, thinking it a cruel and dangerous sport, had prevented him from doing it.

"Pyotr, buy yourself hounds," she moaned.

He dropped the blind and went up to the bed, and would have said something; but at that moment the pain came back, and Olga Mikhalovna uttered an unseemly, piercing scream.

The pain and the constant screaming and moaning stupefied her. She heard, saw, and sometimes spoke, but hardly understood anything, and was only conscious that she was in pain or was just going to be in pain. It seemed to her that the name-day party had been long, long ago—not yesterday, but a year ago perhaps; and that her new life of agony had lasted longer than her childhood, her school-days, her time at the University, and her marriage, and would go on for a long, long time, endlessly. She saw them bring tea to the midwife, and summon her at midday to lunch and afterwards to dinner; she saw Pyotr Dmitrich grow used to coming in, standing for long intervals by the window, and going out again; saw strange men, the maid, Varvara, come in as though they were at home. . . . Varvara said nothing but, "He will, he will," and was angry when anyone closed the drawers and the chest. Olga Mikhalovna saw the light change in the room and in the windows: at one time it was twilight, then thick like fog, then bright daylight as it had been at dinner-time the day before, then again twilight . . . and each of these changes lasted as long as her childhood, her school-days, her life at the University . . .

In the evening two doctors—one bony, bald, with a big red beard; the other with a swarthy Jewish face and cheap spectacles—performed some sort of operation on Olga Mikhalovna. To these unknown men touching her body she felt utterly indifferent. By now she had no feeling of shame, no will, and anyone might do what he would with her. If anyone had rushed at her with a knife, or had insulted Pyotr Dmitrich, or had robbed her of her right to the little creature, she would not have said a word.

They gave her chloroform during the operation. When she came to again, the pain was still there and insufferable. It was night. And Olga Mikhalovna remembered that there had been just such a night with the stillness, the lamp, with the midwife sitting motionless by the bed, with the drawers of the chest pulled out, with Pyotr Dmitrich standing by the window, but some time very, very long ago . . .

V

"I am not dead . . ." thought Olga Mikhalovna when she began to understand her surroundings again, and when the pain was over.

A bright summer day looked in at the widely open windows; in the garden below the windows, the sparrows and the magpies never ceased chattering for one instant.

The drawers were shut now, her husband's bed had been made. There was no sign of the midwife or of the maid, or of Varvara in the room, only Pyotr Dmitrich was standing, as before, motionless by the window looking into the garden. There was no sound of a child's crying, no one was congratulating her or rejoicing, it was evident that the little creature had not been born alive.

"Pyotr!" Olga Mikhalovna called to her husband.

Pyotr Dmitrich looked round. It seemed as though a long time must have passed since the last guest had departed and Olga Mikhalovna had insulted her husband, for Pyotr Dmitrich was perceptibly thinner and hollow-eyed.

"What is it?" he asked, coming up to the bed.

He looked away, moved his lips, and smiled with childlike helplessness.

"Is it all over?" asked Olga Mikhalovna.

Pyotr Dmitrich tried to make some answer, but his lips quivered and his mouth worked like a toothless old man's, like Uncle Nikolai Nikolaich's.

"Olya," he said, wringing his hands; big tears suddenly dropping from his eyes. "Olya, I don't care about your property qualification, nor the Circuit Courts . . ." (he gave a sob) "nor particular views, nor those visitors, nor your fortune. . . . I don't care about anything! Why didn't we take care of our child? Oh, it's no good talking!"

With a despairing gesture he went out of the bedroom.[3]

---

[3] Chekhov deleted this text from the final version of the story:

In a little while he again went in, took something off the table and, not looking once at his wife, went out the other door.

"You're leaving, doctor?" he asked loudly from the door and in such a tone as if he were speaking with a bailiff or witness. "One job finished and you take on another? Right? Each plowman has his field. . . . Each has to labor. . . ."

He was probably giving the doctor his fee, because the doctor said shyly, "No need to worry. . . ."

"What's that? Every job needs its reward . . . I am very grateful, doctor! I ask you not to forget us sinners. . . ."

The word "grateful" Pyotr Dmitrich said like this: "gra-a-til." But neither by his voice, nor by his tone, nor by his heavy, steady walk, was it possible to guess that this man, a minute ago, was crying! Having seen the doctor out, Pyotr Dmitrich quickly walked through the bedroom to his office. Passing by his wife, he looked at her tenderly, guiltily, and imploringly. It was as if he wanted to tell her: "I can't not lie! I don't have the strength to fight myself. Help me!"

But nothing mattered to Olga Mikhalovna now; there was a mistiness in her brain from the chloroform, an emptiness in her soul. . . .

The dull indifference to life which had overcome her when the two doctors were performing the operation still had possession of her.

AFTER THE THEATER

(*После Театра*, 1892)

In this little story, made shorter and finer through Chekhov's revisions after its first publication, we meet a teenager whose imagination has leaped ahead of her experience. Sixteen-year-old Nadya is inspired by Russian literature's most romantic heroine, Tatyana in Alexander Pushkin's Eugene Onegin, *as dramatized in the opera by Chekhov's friend Peter Ilyich Tchaikovsky. Nadya induces overwhelming feelings in herself as she contemplates two suitors: "Nadya laid her arms on the table and bent her head to them, and her hair covered over the letter. She remembered that the student Gruzdev also loved her and that he had as much right to her letter as Gorny. In which case, wouldn't it be better to write to Gruzdev? For no reason at all, joyfulness stirred in her chest: at first the joyfulness was small and rolled around in her chest like a rubber ball, and then it got wider, bigger and surged like a wave."*

NADYA ZELENINA, HAVING returned with her mother from the theater, where they were playing *Eugene Onegin*, and having gone to her room, quickly took off her dress, let down her hair, and in only her skirt and white blouse, sat herself as soon as possible at her table in order to write a letter like Tatyana's.

"I love you," she wrote, "but you don't love me, you don't."

She wrote that and laughed.

She was only sixteen and so far was not in love with anybody. She knew that the officer Gorny and the student Gruzdev loved her, but now, after the opera, she wanted to doubt their love. To be unloved and unhappy—how interesting! When one loves a lot and the other is indifferent, there is something beautiful, touching, and poetic about it. Onegin is interesting because he is not in love, and Tatyana is fascinating because she is very much in love, but if they loved each other equally and were happy, they would probably seem boring.

"Stop declaring that you love me," Nadya continued to write, thinking about the officer Gorny. "I can't believe you. You're very intelligent, educated, serious, you have enormous talent and perhaps you're expecting a brilliant future, but I'm an uninteresting, insignificant girl, and you yourself know very well that I would only be a hindrance in your life. True, you were carried away by me, and you thought you had met your ideal in me, but that was a mistake, and now you're asking yourself in despair: 'Why did I meet this girl?' And it's only your kindness that prevents your acknowledging this! . . ."

Nadya began feeling sorry for herself and started to cry and continued:

"I would just put on a nun's habit and go wherever my eyes led me, if it wasn't hard for me to abandon my mother and brother. But you would be free and would love another. Oh, if I were dead!"

Through her tears it was impossible to decipher what had been written; on the table, on the floor, and on the ceiling tiny rainbows were quivering, as if Nadya were looking through a prism. It was impossible to write; she leaned back into the armchair and thought about Gorny.

My God, how interesting, how fascinating men are! Nadya remembered what a beautiful expression the officer had, how ingratiating, guilty, and soft it was when people argued with him about music, and how he made an effort so that his voice wouldn't sound passionate. In society, where a cool high-toned indifference is counted a sign of a good upbringing and noble manners, one hides one's passions. And he hides his, but he's unsuccessful as everyone well knows that he passionately loves music. Endless arguments about music and bold judgments by ignorant people hold him in a constant tension; he's frightened, shy, silent. He plays the piano marvelously, like a genuine pianist, and if he weren't an officer he would probably be a famous musician.

The tears dried on her eyes. Nadya remembered that Gorny declared his love to her at the symphony concert and then again near the cloakroom where a draft blew from all sides.

"I'm very glad that, finally, you met the student Gruzdev," she continued writing. "He's a very smart person and you will surely like him. He was with us yesterday until two o'clock in the morning. All of us were in ecstasies, and I regretted that you hadn't come to us. He said so many remarkable things."

Nadya laid her arms on the table and bent her head to them, and her hair covered over the letter. She remembered that the student Gruzdev also loved her and that he had as much right to her letter as Gorny. In which case, wouldn't it be better to write to Gruzdev? For no reason at all, joyfulness stirred in her chest: at first the joyfulness was small and rolled around in her chest like a rubber ball, and then it got wider, bigger, and surged like a wave. Nadya had already forgotten about Gorny and Gruzdev, her thoughts got tangled up, and the joyfulness grew and grew; from her chest it went into her arms and legs and it seemed like a light cool breeze was blowing across her head and rustling her hair. Her shoulders quivered with quiet laughter, and the table quivered and so did the glass over the lamp, and the tears from her eyes spattered on the letter. She wasn't able to stop this laughter and in order to show herself that she wasn't laughing without reason she hurried to remember something funny.

"What a funny poodle!" she said, feeling that she was suffocating from laughter. "What a funny poodle!"

She remembered how last night after tea Gruzdev played with Maxim the poodle and then told about a very smart poodle who chased a raven in the yard, but the raven looked around at him and said,

"Ah, you rascal!"

Not knowing he was dealing with an educated raven, the poodle was terribly confused and stepped back in perplexity, and then started barking.

"No, it will be better for me to love Gruzdev," decided Nadya, and she tore up the letter.

She began thinking about the student, about his love, about her love, and it turned out that the thoughts in her head flowed apart and she thought about everything: about Mama, about the street, about the pencil, about the piano. . . . She was thinking joyfully and found that all was well, marvelous, and the joyfulness told her that this was still not everything, that in a short time it would be even better. Soon it would be spring, summer, traveling with Mama to Gorbinka; Gorny would go on leave, he would stroll with her in the garden and woo her. Gruzdev too will come. He'll play croquet with her and skittles, and tell her funny things or amazing things. She passionately longed for the garden, darkness, clear skies, stars. Again her shoulders quivered with laughter and it seemed to her that she smelled wormwood in the room and as if a branch was knocking at the window.

She went to her bed and sat, not knowing what to do with the great joy that was tormenting her; she looked at the ikon hanging over the head of the bed and said:

"O Lord, O Lord, O Lord!"

ABOUT LOVE

(*О Любви*, 1898)

Alekhin is a landowner passing the time at his home with two friends who have been out hunting. He tells of an extreme personal experience—romantic restraint: "And each time I went into town I could see from her eyes that she was expecting me, and indeed she would confess to me she had had a strange feeling all that day and had guessed that I would be coming. We would alternate long periods of talking with periods of silence, but we never acknowledged our love for each other, timidly and jealously concealing it. We were afraid of everything that might bring our secret out in the open even to ourselves. I loved her tenderly, deeply, but I kept analyzing the situation and asking myself what dire repercussions our love might have if we failed to find the strength to fight against it. My love was so gentle and so sad; and I could not conceive of it being the means for the abrupt interruption of the calm happy life of her husband and children, and this whole household in which everyone loved and trusted me. How could this be honorable?"

This excellent translation by Lydia Razran Stone, based on Constance Garnett's translation, was first published in the Fall 2010 issue of Chtenia: Readings from Russia, *edited by Paul Richardson. "About Love" is the third in a trilogy of stories by Chekhov, following "The Man in a Case" and "Gooseberries."*

NEXT DAY AT lunch the guests were served some very tasty pies, crayfish, and mutton cutlets. While they were eating, Nikanor, the cook, came in to ask what they would like for dinner. He was a man of medium height with a puffy face and small eyes. He was clean shaven, but it looked as though the hair on his face had been plucked out rather than shaved off.

Alekhin told his visitors that the beautiful Pelagea was in love with this cook. Since Nikanor drank heavily and tended to get violent, she did not want to marry him, but was willing simply to live with him. He, however, was very religious, and his convictions would not allow him to live in sin. He demanded that she marry him and would hear of nothing else, and when he got drunk he used to curse and threatened her and even beat her. Whenever this happened she hid in the upstairs story, sobbing, and on such occasions Alekhin and his servants stayed in the house so they could protect her if necessary.

The men began to discuss love.

"The question of what gives rise to love," remarked Alekhin, "for example, why Pelagea doesn't love somebody more like she is in character and appearance, but instead falls for Nikanor, with his ugly snout (that's what we all call him, 'Snout') or how much personal happiness matters to love—the answers to such questions are completely unknown. Everyone is free to think whatever he wants about them. So far only one indisputable truth has been spoken about love: 'This is a great mystery.' Everything else that has ever been written or said about love is not an answer or solution, but only a restatement of questions that still remain unanswered. The explanation that would seem to fit one case does not apply in a dozen others, and the very best thing, to my mind, would be to explain every case individually without attempting to generalize. We ought, as the doctors say, to individualize each case."

"Absolutely right," Burkin assented.

"We educated Russians are partial to questions that cannot be answered. Love is normally poeticized, decorated with roses, and nightingales. In addition, Russians like us decorate our love with these portentous questions, and, furthermore, always choose to dwell on the least interesting among them. When I was a student in Moscow, I had a mistress, a charming woman, and every time I held her in my arms she was thinking about how much housekeeping money I would give her that month and what the going price for a pound of beef was. In the same way, when we are in love, we never cease asking ourselves questions of a certain type: whether our love is honorable or dishonorable, rational or stupid, what it is leading to, and so on. Whether this is a good thing or not

I don't know, but I do know that it gets in the way and makes us dissatisfied and irritable."

These words seemed to be leading up to a story he wanted to tell. People who live alone always have something stored up inside that they are eager to talk about. In town bachelors visit the public baths and restaurants in order to talk and sometimes tell the bath attendants and waiters the most interesting stories. People who live in the country, as a rule, unburden themselves to their houseguests. Outside the window the sky was gray, the trees were drenched with rain; in this weather the men had no wish to leave the house, and so there was nothing left to do but tell and listen to stories.

"I have lived at Sofino and occupied myself with farming for quite a long time," Alekhin began, "ever since I left the University. My education prepared me to do anything but manual labor and my temperament predisposes me to intellectual pursuits, but when I came home from the university, there was a large debt outstanding on our estate, which my father had mortgaged partially to pay for my expensive education. I decided that I would not leave here until I had paid off this debt. I made this resolve and began working, I confess, not without some feeling of distaste. The soil here is not very fertile and, to keep from losing money on the crops, you either have to rely on the labor of serfs or hired hands (which is virtually the same thing) or work the land the way the peasants do, that is work in the field yourself with your family. There is no middle ground. But at first I did not bother with such fine distinctions. I did not leave a clod of earth unturned; I rounded up all the peasants, men and women both, from the neighboring villages and put them to work. And work we did; at a furious pace. I myself plowed and sowed and reaped. And I was bored every minute of the time, screwing up my face fastidiously like a cat forced by hunger to eat cucumbers from the kitchen-garden. My whole body ached, and I was continually falling asleep on my feet. At the beginning I thought I could easily live this life of hard labor while retaining my cultured habits, if I could only maintain a certain external order in my life. Thus, I established myself upstairs here in the best rooms, and had the servants bring my coffee and liqueur to me up there after lunch and dinner. I would read *Vestnik Yevropy* every night before I went to sleep. But one day our priest, Father Ivan, dropped by and polished off my entire stock of liqueur at a single go. Then I gave my copies of *Vestnik Yevropy* to the priest's daughters, since in summer, especially during haymaking,

I never made it to my bed at all, but fell asleep in a sledge in the barn, or somewhere in the forester's lodge. What chance did I have to read? Little by little I moved downstairs and began dining in the servants' kitchen, and now nothing is left of my former luxury but the servants I cannot bear to let go because they were in my father's service.

"Not long after I settled here, I was made an honorary member of the magistrate's court. From time to time I would have to go into town to attend sessions of the district congress or court, which made a pleasant break for me. When you spend two or three months cooped up in the country without going anywhere, especially in the winter, you start to long for the sight of a black frock coat. And these sessions showed me frock-coats, and uniforms, and dress-coats, too. The members of the court were lawyers, educated men with whom I could have real discussions. After sleeping in the sledge and eating my meals in the kitchen, to sit in an armchair in clean linen, and dress shoes, with a chain of office around my neck was quite a luxury!

I received a warm welcome in the town and was very eager to make new acquaintances. Of all those I met, the one I knew and, to tell the truth, liked the best was Luganovich, the vice-president of the court. I think both of you know him, the nicest fellow you'd ever hope to meet. You remember the famous arson case we had? Well, the preliminary investigation lasted two days. The whole court was exhausted. Luganovich looked at me and said:

" 'You know what, why don't you come and have dinner at my house?'

"This was unexpected, since my acquaintance with Luganovich had been strictly professional and I had never been to his house before. I went to my hotel room and took a minute or two to change my clothes and off I went to dinner. And there I had the opportunity to get to know Anna Alekseyevna, Luganovich's wife. At that time she was still very young, no more than twenty-two; her first child had been born only six months before. It is all a thing of the past; and now I find it difficult to define what exactly there was about her that I found so exceptional, that attracted me so much. But that time, at that first dinner, the reasons were overwhelmingly clear to me. I saw a young woman beautiful, good-hearted, intelligent, and enchanting, whose equal I had never before encountered. Immediately I felt I had some sort of bond with her. She seemed familiar to me, as if I had seen that face, those friendly, intelligent eyes, sometime during my childhood; perhaps in the album my mother kept on her dresser.

"Four Jews had been charged with arson, and they had been tried as a criminal gang, which I thought was completely unfounded. During dinner my mind was still on this case that had disturbed me a great deal; I can't tell you what I myself said, but I do remember that Anna Alekseyevna kept shaking her head and saying to her husband:

" 'Dmitry, how could this have happened?'

"Luganovich is a good soul, but he is one of those naive people who are firmly of the opinion that once someone has been brought before a court, he must be guilty, and that the only way it is permissible to question the verdict is on paper, following due legal procedures, and not over dinner in a private conversation.

" 'Well, you and I, for example are innocent of arson,' he said mildly, 'and so no one has tried us for it or sent us to prison.'

"And both of them—husband and wife—kept urging me to have more to eat and drink. Certain trifling details that I observed, the way they made the coffee together, for instance, and the way they understood each other's thoughts before a sentence was completed made me think that that they had a close and happy marriage and were pleased to have visitors. After dinner they played a duet on the piano; then it got dark, and I went home. That was in early spring.

"I spent the entire following summer at Sofino without a break and had no time to think about life in town, but I carried the memory of the slender fair-haired woman with me throughout that period. I did not really think about her, but it was as though a faint shadow of her was always present in my mind.

"In late autumn I attended a theatrical performance in town, a charity benefit. I had been invited to visit the governor's box during the intermission and when I did, I saw Anna Alekseyevna sitting beside the governor's wife. Once again I had the sudden, overwhelming impression of beauty and warm, understanding eyes, and again the same feeling that there was a bond between us. We sat side by side for a while and then went out into the lobby.

" 'You've grown thinner,' she said; 'have you been ill?'

" 'Yes, I've had rheumatism in my shoulder, and in rainy weather I sleep badly.'

" 'You look run down. In the spring, when you came to dinner, you were younger, more confident. You were full of eagerness then, and talked a great deal; you were very interesting, and I confess you made quite an impression on me. For some reason you often popped into my memory during the summer, and as I was getting ready for the theater today I thought I was likely to see you.'

"And she laughed.

" 'But you look run down today,' she repeated; 'it makes you seem older.'

"The next day I lunched at the Luganoviches'. After lunch they were going to drive to their summer place, in order to make arrangements for the winter, and I accompanied them. We returned to town together, and, at midnight I was drinking tea with them in quiet domestic surroundings while the fire glowed, and the young mother kept leaving the room to make sure her little girl was asleep. And after that when I went to town, I never failed to visit the Luganoviches. They grew used to me, and I grew used to them. As a rule I would enter their house unannounced, like one of the family.

" 'Who is there?' she would call from one of the inner rooms far off in the light drawl that I found so attractive.

" 'It's Pavel Konstantinovich,' the maid or nanny would answer.

"Anna Alekseyevna would come out to me with a worried face, and would ask me every time, 'Why has it been so long since you were here? Did something happen?'

"Her eyes, the graceful, aristocratic-looking hand that she offered me, her everyday dress, the way she did her hair, her voice, her step, always produced the same impression on me that there was something new and extraordinary in my life, something important. We would talk for hours, or we would sit in silence, each thinking his own thoughts, or she would play the piano for me. If I found no one at home I stayed and waited, chatting with the nanny, playing with the child, or lying on the Turkish sofa in the study reading a newspaper. When Anna Alekseyevna came back I would meet her in the front hall and take her parcels from her; and, for some reason, I would carry those parcels every time with the kind of great love and great solemnity a boy would feel.

"There is a proverb that says that if a peasant woman has nothing to fret over, she goes out and buys a pig. So too it seemed that the Luganoviches had had nothing to fret over, so they made friends with me. If I did not come to town for a while, they were sure I was sick or something else had happened to me, and they both became extremely anxious. They worried that I, an educated man with a knowledge of languages, instead of devoting myself to science or literary pursuits, was living in the country, running around like a squirrel in a wheel, working like a dog, and never had a penny to show for it. They imagined that I was unhappy and that I only talked, laughed, and ate to conceal my suffering. Even when I was enjoying myself and did indeed feel happy I was aware of their searching eyes fixed upon me. They were particularly touching when I really was in a bad state, when a creditor was pressuring me or I did not have the money to pay my mortgage on time. The two of them, husband and wife, would go off to the window and whisper together; then Luganovich would come to me and say with a serious expression on his face:

" 'If you currently are in need of some money, Pavel Konstantinovich, my wife and I beg you not to hesitate to borrow from us.'

"And he would blush to his ears with emotion. Other times, after they had whispered in the same way at the window, he would come up to me, again with red ears, and say:

" 'My wife and I earnestly beg you to accept this present.'

"And he would give me cufflinks, a cigarette case, or a lamp, and in return I would send them game, butter, and flowers from the country. I should mention here that they both had considerable money of their own. When I had first moved here, I often borrowed money, and was not very fastidious about it—I borrowed wherever I could—but nothing in the world would have induced me to borrow from the Luganoviches. But why talk of money?

"I was indeed unhappy. In my house, in the barn, I was always thinking about her. I kept trying to figure out why a beautiful, intelligent young woman would marry a someone who was not particularly interesting and nearly an old man (her husband was past forty) and bear his children. I would ponder the mystery of how this undistinguished though good-hearted and straightforward man, this man with a simple outlook on life whose opinions were so boring and commonsensical, who sat out dances at parties among the solid citizens, listless and unsought after with a passive indifferent expression as if he were at a business meeting, could yet believe in his right to be happy, to have children with her. I kept trying to understand why she had met him, and not me, first and how such a terrible mistake had been allowed to occur in our lives.

"And each time I went into town I could see from her eyes that she was expecting me, and indeed she would confess to me she had had a strange feeling all that day and had guessed that I would be coming. We would alternate long periods of talking with periods of silence, but we never acknowledged our love for each other, timidly and jealously concealing it. We were afraid of everything that might bring our secret out in the open even to ourselves. I loved her tenderly, deeply, but I kept analyzing the situation and asking myself what dire repercussions our love might have if we failed to find the strength to fight against it. My love was so gentle and so sad; and I could not conceive of it being the means for the abrupt interruption of the calm happy life of her husband and children, and this whole household in which everyone loved and trusted me. How could this be honorable? She would have to go away with me, but where? Where could I take her? It would have been something else entirely if I had had been leading a wonderful, interesting life—if, for instance, I had been working for the emancipation of my country, or was a celebrated scientist, artist or painter; but I simply would be taking her from one unexceptional prosaic life to another, equally as prosaic, if not more so. And how long would our happiness last? What would happen to her if I were to become ill, or die, or if we simply stopped loving each other?

"And she apparently had been thinking along similar lines. She considered her husband, her children, and her mother, who loved Luganovich like a son. If she had given in to her feelings for me she would either have had to lie, or else tell the truth, and in her position either alternative would have been equally terrible and painful. And, too, she was tormented by the question of whether her love would bring me happiness. Would she not complicate my life, which, as it was, was hard enough and full of all sorts of trouble? She imagined that she was not young enough for me, that she was not hardworking or energetic enough to begin a new life, and she often talked to her husband about how I needed to marry a girl of intelligence and character who would be a good homemaker and helpmate to me—and then she would immediately add that it if you searched the whole town you would be unlikely to find even one such girl.

"Meanwhile the years were passing. Anna Alekseyevna already had two children. When I arrived at the Luganoviches' the servants smiled cordially, the children shouted that Uncle Pavel

Konstantinovich had come and hung on my neck; everyone was delighted. They did not understand what was going on in my soul, and thought that I, too, was happy. Everyone looked on me as a noble being. The adults and children alike felt that a noble being was walking about their rooms, and this gave a special charm to their manner towards me, as though my presence there made their lives, too, purer and more beautiful. Anna Alekseyevna and I used to go to the theater together; we always went on foot and sat side by side in the stalls, our shoulders touching. I would take the opera-glass from her hands without a word, and I would feel at that minute that we were truly joined together, that she was mine, that we could not live without each other. Yet, through some strange misunderstanding, each time we emerged from the theater we said goodbye and parted as though we were mere acquaintances. People in town had already begun to talk about us, saying God knows what, but there was not a word of truth in any of it!

"After some years passed, Anna Alekseyevna started to go away on frequent visits to her mother or sister; and began to be moody. At times she suffered, feeling that she was not satisfied with her life, and even that her life was ruined. And at those times she felt reluctant to be in the presence of her husband and children. She had begun to be treated for depression.

"We maintained our silence, and in the presence of outsiders she displayed a strange irritation with me: she disagreed with whatever I said and if I got into a dispute she would always take the other person's side. If I dropped something, she would say coldly:

" 'I congratulate you.'

"If I forgot to bring along the opera-glasses when we went to the theater, she would say afterwards:

" 'I just knew you would forget them.'

"Luckily or unluckily, there is nothing in our lives that does not eventually come to an end. The time came when we had to part. Luganovich had been appointed chairman of a court in one of the western provinces. They had to sell their furniture, their horses, and their summer house. We drove out to the summer house, and on the way back, when we turned around for one last look at the garden and the green roof, we were all sad and I realized that it was not just the house I was saying goodbye to. It had been decided that, in late August, Anna Alekseyevna would go off to the Crimea, at her doctor's recommendation, and Luganovich and the children would set off for the western province a little after that.

"A large crowd turned out to see Anna Alekseyevna off. When she had already said goodbye to her husband and her children and there was only a minute left before the third bell, I ran into her compartment to put a basket, which she had almost forgotten, on the rack, and I too had to say goodbye. When our eyes met in the compartment our will power deserted us both; I took her in my arms, she pressed her face to my chest and wept, I kissed her face, her shoulders, and her hands wet with tears—oh, how wretched we were!—I confessed my love for her, and, with a burning pain in my heart, I realized how unnecessary, petty, and illusory was everything that had gotten in the way of our love. I understood that when you love you must either base all the decisions and judgments you make about that love on what is its most exalted aspect, what is more important than happiness or unhappiness, sin or virtue in their accepted meaning, or you must keep from making decisions and judgments at all.

"I kissed her for the last time, pressed her hand, and we parted forever. The train had already started. I went into the next compartment—it was empty—and sat there weeping until we reached the next station. Then I walked home to Sofino. . . ."

While Alekhin was telling his story, the rain stopped and the sun came out. Burkin and Ivan Ivanich went out onto the balcony, from which there was a beautiful view over the garden and the mill pond, which now was shining in the sun like a mirror. They admired it, and at the same time they were sorry that this man with the kind, understanding eyes, who had told them this story with such genuine feeling, should be rushing round and round this huge estate like a squirrel in a wheel instead of devoting himself to science or something else that would have made his life more pleasant; and they thought what a sorrowful face Anna Alekseyevna must have had when he said goodbye to her in the railway-carriage and kissed her face and shoulders. Both of them had met her in the town, and Burkin was acquainted with her and thought her beautiful.

THE DARLING

(*Душечка*, 1899)

Chekhov jotted an idea in his notebook: "There was a wife of an artist—she loved the theater, writers. It seemed she completely went in for the business of her husband, and everyone was amazed how fortunately he had married; but then he died; she marries a confectioner, and it seems there's nothing she loves so much as making jam, and already holds theater in contempt, just as if it's a religion to emulate her husband." Four or five years later, he wrote "The Darling," one of his most popular stories. Leo Tolstoy, the grandest figure in Russian literature, who influenced every Russian writer of his time—including Chekhov, whom he befriended— loved reading this story aloud to his family and visitors. A guest of Tolstoy's recalled: "In the comic places he sometimes laughed to tears, and in the touching places he poured out tears."[1]

This translation is by Thomas Seltzer, a Russian native and language wizard who moved to America as a boy and became a prominent editor and publisher; he included "The Darling" in Best Russian Short Stories *(1917).*

OLENKA, THE DAUGHTER of the retired collegiate assessor Plemyanikov, was sitting on the back-door steps of her house doing nothing. It was hot, the flies were nagging and teasing, and it was pleasant to think that it would soon be evening. Dark rain clouds were gathering from the east, wafting a breath of moisture every now and then.

---

[1] Anton Chekhov, *Polnoe Sobranie Sochineniy i Pisem: Sobraniya*, Tom 10 [Collected Works and Letters: Works, Vol. 10] (Moscow: Nauka, 1974), 410.

Kukin, who roomed in the wing of the same house, was standing in the yard looking up at the sky. He was the manager of the Tivoli, an open-air theater.

"Again," he said despairingly. "Rain again. Rain, rain, rain! Every day rain! As though to spite me. I might as well stick my head into a noose and be done with it. It's ruining me. Heavy losses every day!" He wrung his hands, and continued, addressing Olenka: "What a life, Olga Semyonovna! It's enough to make a man weep. He works, he does his best, his very best, he tortures himself, he passes sleepless nights, he thinks and thinks and thinks how to do everything just right. And what's the result? He gives the public the best operetta, the very best pantomime, excellent artists. But do they want it? Have they the least appreciation of it? The public is rude. The public is a great boor. The public wants a circus, a lot of nonsense, a lot of stuff. And there's the weather. Look! Rain almost every evening. It began to rain on the tenth of May, and it's kept it up through the whole of June. It's simply awful. I can't get any audiences, and don't I have to pay rent? Don't I have to pay the actors?"

The next day towards evening the clouds gathered again, and Kukin said with an hysterical laugh:

"Oh, I don't care. Let it do its worst. Let it drown the whole theater, and me, too. All right, no luck for me in this world or the next. Let the actors bring suit against me and drag me to court. What's the court? Why not Siberia at hard labor, or even the scaffold? Ha, ha, ha!"

It was the same on the third day.

Olenka listened to Kukin seriously, in silence. Sometimes tears would rise to her eyes. At last Kukin's misfortune touched her. She fell in love with him. He was short, gaunt, with a yellow face, and curly hair combed back from his forehead, and a thin tenor voice. His features puckered all up when he spoke. Despair was ever inscribed on his face. And yet he awakened in Olenka a sincere, deep feeling.

She was always loving somebody. She couldn't get on without loving somebody. She had loved her sick father, who sat the whole time in his armchair in a darkened room, breathing heavily. She had loved her aunt, who came from Brianska once or twice a year to visit them. And before that, when a pupil at school, she had loved her French teacher. She was a quiet, kind-hearted, compassionate girl, with a soft gentle way about her. And she made a very healthy, wholesome impression. Looking at her full, rosy cheeks, at her soft white neck with the black mole, and at the good, naïve smile that always played on her face when something pleasant was said, the men would think, "Not so bad," and would smile too; and the lady visitors, in the middle of the conversation, would suddenly grasp her hand and exclaim, "You darling!" in a burst of delight.

The house, hers by inheritance, in which she had lived from birth, was located at the outskirts of the city on the Gypsy Road, not far from the Tivoli. From early evening till late at night she could hear the music in the theater and the bursting of the rockets; and it seemed to her that Kukin was roaring and battling with his fate and taking his chief enemy, the indifferent public, by assault. Her heart melted softly, she felt no desire to sleep, and when Kukin returned home towards morning, she tapped on her window-pane, and through the curtains he saw her face and one shoulder and the kind smile she gave him.

He proposed to her, and they were married. And when he had a good look of her neck and her full vigorous shoulders, he clapped his hands and said:

"You darling!"

He was happy. But it rained on their wedding-day, and the expression of despair never left his face.

They got along well together. She sat in the cashier's box, kept the theater in order, wrote down the expenses, and paid out the salaries. Her rosy cheeks, her kind, naïve smile, like a halo around her face, could be seen at the cashier's window, behind the scenes, and in the café. She began to tell her friends that the theater was the greatest, the most important, the most essential thing in the world, that it was the only place to obtain true enjoyment in and become humanized and educated.

"But do you suppose the public appreciates it?" she asked. "What the public wants is the circus. Yesterday Vanichka and I gave *Faust Burlesqued*, and almost all the boxes were empty. If we had given some silly nonsense, I assure you, the theater would have been overcrowded. Tomorrow we'll put on *Orpheus in Hades*. Do come."

Whatever Kukin said about the theater and the actors, she repeated. She spoke, as he did, with contempt of the public, of its indifference to art, of its boorishness. She meddled in the rehearsals, corrected the actors, watched the conduct of the musicians; and when an unfavorable criticism appeared in the local paper, she wept and went to the editor to argue with him.

The actors were fond of her and called her "Vanichka and I" and "the darling." She was sorry for them and lent them small sums. When they cheated her, she never complained to her husband; at the most she shed a few tears.

In winter, too, they got along nicely together. They leased a theater in the town for the whole winter and sublet it for short periods to a Little Russian theatrical company, to a conjuror, and to the local amateur players.

Olenka grew fuller and was always beaming with contentment; while Kukin grew thinner and yellower and complained of his terrible losses, though he did fairly well the whole winter. At night he coughed, and she gave him raspberry syrup and lime water, rubbed him with *eau de Cologne*, and wrapped him up in soft coverings.

"You are my precious sweet," she said with perfect sincerity, stroking his hair. "You are such a dear."

At Lent he went to Moscow to get his company together, and, while without him, Olenka was unable to sleep. She sat at the window the whole time, gazing at the stars. She likened herself to the hens that are also uneasy and unable to sleep when their rooster is out of the coop. Kukin was detained in Moscow. He wrote he would be back during Easter Week, and in his letters discussed arrangements already for the Tivoli. But late one night, before Easter Monday, there was an ill-omened knocking at the wicket-gate. It was like a knocking on a barrel—boom, boom, boom! The sleepy cook ran barefooted, splashing through the puddles, to open the gate.

"Open the gate, please," said someone in a hollow bass voice. "I have a telegram for you."

Olenka had received telegrams from her husband before; but this time, somehow, she was numbed with terror. She opened the telegram with trembling hands and read:

"Ivan Petrovich died suddenly today. Awaiting propt orders for wuneral Tuesday."

That was the way the telegram was written—"wuneral"—and another unintelligible word—"propt." The telegram was signed by the manager of the opera company.

"My dearest!" Olenka burst out sobbing. "Vanichka, my dearest, my sweetheart. Why did I ever meet you? Why did I ever get to know you and love you? To whom have you abandoned your poor Olenka, your poor, unhappy Olenka?"

Kukin was buried on Tuesday in the Vagankov Cemetery in Moscow. Olenka returned home on Wednesday; and as soon as she entered her house she threw herself on her bed and broke into such loud sobbing that she could be heard in the street and in the neighboring yards.

"The darling!" said the neighbors, crossing themselves. "How Olga Semyonovna, the poor darling, is grieving!"

Three months afterwards Olenka was returning home from mass, downhearted and in deep mourning. Beside her walked a man also returning from church, Vasily Pustovalov, the manager of the merchant Babakayev's lumberyard. He was wearing a straw hat, a white vest with a gold chain, and looked more like a landowner than a businessman.

"Everything has its ordained course, Olga Semyonovna," he said sedately, with sympathy in his voice. "And if anyone near and dear to us dies, then it means it was God's will and we should remember that and bear it with submission."

He took her to the wicket-gate, said goodbye, and went away. After that she heard his sedate voice the whole day; and on closing her eyes she instantly had a vision of his dark beard. She took a great liking to him. And evidently he had been impressed by her, too; for, not long after, an elderly woman, a distant acquaintance, came in to have a cup of coffee with her. As soon as the woman was seated at the table she began to speak about Pustovalov—how good he was, what a steady man, and any woman could be glad to get him as a husband. Three days later Pustovalov himself paid Olenka a visit. He stayed only about ten minutes, and spoke little, but Olenka fell in love with him, fell in love so desperately that she did not sleep the whole night and burned as with fever. In the morning she sent for the elderly woman. Soon after, Olenka and Pustovalov were engaged, and the wedding followed.

Pustovalov and Olenka lived happily together. He usually stayed in the lumberyard until dinner, then went out on business. In his absence Olenka took his place in the office until evening, attending to the book-keeping and despatching the orders.

"Lumber rises twenty percent every year nowadays," she told her customers and acquaintances. "Imagine, we used to buy wood from our forests here. Now Vasichka has to go every year to the government of Mogilev to get wood. And the taxes!" she exclaimed, covering her cheeks with her hands in terror. "What taxes!"

She felt as if she had been dealing in lumber for ever so long, that the most important and essential thing in life was lumber. There was something touching and endearing in the way she pronounced the words, "beam," "joist," "plank," "stave," "lath," "gun-carriage," "clamp." At night she dreamed of whole mountains of boards and planks, long, endless rows of wagons conveying the wood somewhere, far, far from the city. She dreamed that a whole regiment of beams, 36 ft. x 5 in., were advancing in an upright position to do battle against the lumber-yard; that the beams and joists and clamps were knocking against each other, emitting the sharp crackling reports of dry wood, that they were all falling and then rising again, piling on top of each other. Olenka cried out in her sleep, and Pustovalov said to her gently:

"Olenka my dear, what is the matter? Cross yourself."

Her husband's opinions were all hers. If he thought the room was too hot, she thought so too. If he thought business was slow, she thought business was slow. Pustovalov was not fond of amusements and stayed home on holidays; she did the same.

"You are always either at home or in the office," said her friends. "Why don't you go to the theater or to the circus, darling?"

"Vasichka and I never go to the theater," she answered sedately. "We have work to do, we have no time for nonsense. What does one get out of going to the theater?"

On Saturdays she and Pustovalov went to vespers, and on holidays to early mass. On returning home they walked side by side with rapt faces, an agreeable smell emanating from both of them and her silk dress rustling pleasantly. At home they drank tea with milk-bread and various jams, and then ate pie. Every day at noontime there was an appetizing odor in the yard and outside the gate of cabbage soup, roast mutton, or duck; and, on fast days, of fish. You couldn't pass the gate without being seized by an acute desire to eat. The samovar was always boiling on the office table, and customers were treated to tea and biscuits. Once a week the married couple went to the baths and returned with red faces, walking side by side.

"We are getting along very well, thank God," said Olenka to her friends. "God grant that all should live as well as Vasichka and I."

When Pustovalov went to the government of Mogilev to buy wood, she was dreadfully homesick for him, did not sleep nights, and cried. Sometimes the veterinary surgeon of the regiment, Smirnov, a young man who lodged in the wing of her house, came to see her evenings. He related incidents, or they played cards together. This distracted her. The most interesting of his stories were those of his own life. He was married and had a son; but he had separated from his wife because she had deceived him, and now he hated her and sent her forty rubles a month for his son's support. Olenka sighed, shook her head, and was sorry for him.

"Well, the Lord keep you," she said, as she saw him off to the door by candlelight. "Thank you for coming to kill time with me. May God give you health. Mother in Heaven!" She spoke very sedately, very judiciously, imitating her husband. The veterinary surgeon had disappeared behind the door when she called out after him: "Do you know, Vladimir Platonych, you ought to make up with your wife. Forgive her, if only for the sake of your son. The child understands everything, you may be sure."

When Pustovalov returned, she told him in a low voice about the veterinary surgeon and his unhappy family life; and they sighed and shook their heads, and talked about the boy who must be homesick for his father. Then, by a strange association of ideas, they both stopped before the sacred images, made genuflections, and prayed to God to send them children.

And so the Pustovalovs lived for full six years, quietly and peaceably, in perfect love and harmony. But once in the winter Vasily Andreyich, after drinking some hot tea, went out into the lumberyard without a hat on his head, caught a cold, and took sick. He was treated by the best physicians, but the malady progressed, and he died after an illness of four months. Olenka was again left a widow.

"To whom have you left me, my darling?" she wailed after the funeral. "How shall I live now without you, wretched creature that I am. Pity me, good people, pity me, fatherless and motherless, all alone in the world!"

She went about dressed in black and weepers, and she gave up wearing hats and gloves for good. She hardly left the house except to go to church and to visit her husband's grave. She almost led the life of a nun.

It was not until six months had passed that she took off the weepers and opened her shutters. She began to go out occasionally in the morning to market with her cook. But how she lived at home and what went on there, could only be surmised. It could be

surmised from the fact that she was seen in her little garden drinking
tea with the veterinarian while he read the paper out loud to her,
and also from the fact that once on meeting an acquaintance at the
post-office, she said to her:

"There is no proper veterinary inspection in our town. That is
why there is so much disease. You constantly hear of people getting
sick from the milk and becoming infected by the horses and cows.
The health of domestic animals ought really to be looked after as
much as that of human beings."

She repeated the veterinarian's words and held the same opinions
as he about everything. It was plain that she could not exist a single
year without an attachment, and she found her new happiness in
the wing of her house. In anyone else this would have been
condemned; but no one could think ill of Olenka. Everything in
her life was so transparent. She and the veterinary surgeon never
spoke about the change in their relations. They tried, in fact, to
conceal it, but unsuccessfully; for Olenka could have no secrets.
When the surgeon's colleagues from the regiment came to see him,
she poured tea, and served the supper, and talked to them about the
cattle plague, the foot and mouth disease, and the municipal
slaughterhouses. The surgeon was dreadfully embarrassed, and after
the visitors had left, he caught her hand and hissed angrily:

"Didn't I ask you not to talk about what you don't understand?
When we doctors discuss things, please don't mix in. It's getting to
be a nuisance."

She looked at him in astonishment and alarm, and asked:

"But, Volodichka, what am I to talk about?"

And she threw her arms round his neck, with tears in her eyes,
and begged him not to be angry. And they were both happy.

But their happiness was of short duration. The veterinary
surgeon went away with his regiment to be gone for good, when
it was transferred to some distant place almost as far as Siberia, and
Olenka was left alone.

Now she was completely alone. Her father had long been dead,
and his armchair lay in the attic covered with dust and minus one
leg. She got thin and homely, and the people who met her on the
street no longer looked at her as they had used to, nor smiled at her.
Evidently her best years were over, past and gone, and a new,
dubious life was to begin which it were better not to think about.

In the evening Olenka sat on the steps and heard the music
playing and the rockets bursting in the Tivoli; but it no longer

aroused any response in her. She looked listlessly into the yard, thought of nothing, wanted nothing, and when night came on, she went to bed and dreamed of nothing but the empty yard. She ate and drank as though by compulsion.

And what was worst of all, she no longer held any opinions. She saw and understood everything that went on around her, but she could not form an opinion about it. She knew of nothing to talk about. And how dreadful not to have opinions! For instance, you see a bottle, or you see that it is raining, or you see a muzhik riding by in a wagon. But what the bottle or the rain or the muzhik are for, or what the sense of them all is, you cannot tell—you cannot tell, not for a thousand rubles. In the days of Kukin and Pustovalov and then of the veterinary surgeon, Olenka had had an explanation for everything, and would have given her opinion freely no matter about what. But now there was the same emptiness in her heart and brain as in her yard. It was as galling and bitter as a taste of wormwood.

Gradually the town grew up all around. The Gypsy Road had become a street, and where the Tivoli and the lumberyard had been, there were now houses and a row of side streets. How quickly time flies! Olenka's house turned gloomy, the roof rusty, the shed slanting. Dock and thistles overgrew the yard. Olenka herself had aged and grown homely. In the summer she sat on the steps, and her soul was empty and dreary and bitter. When she caught the breath of spring, or when the wind wafted the chime of the cathedral bells, a sudden flood of memories would pour over her, her heart would expand with a tender warmth, and the tears would stream down her cheeks. But that lasted only a moment. Then would come emptiness again, and the feeling, *What is the use of living?* The black kitten Bryska rubbed up against her and purred softly, but the little creature's caresses left Olenka untouched. That was not what she needed. What she needed was a love that would absorb her whole being, her reason, her whole soul, that would give her ideas, an object in life, that would warm her aging blood. And she shook the black kitten off her skirt angrily, saying:

"Go away! What are you doing here?"

And so day after day, year after year not a single joy, not a single opinion. Whatever Marva, the cook, said was all right.

One hot day in July, towards evening, as the town cattle were being driven by, and the whole yard was filled with clouds of dust, there was suddenly a knocking at the gate. Olenka herself went to open it, and was dumbfounded to behold the veterinarian Smirnov. He had turned gray and was dressed as a civilian. All the old memories flooded into her soul, she could not restrain herself, she burst out crying, and laid her head on Smirnov's breast without saying a word. So overcome was she that she was totally unconscious of how they walked into the house and seated themselves to drink tea.

"My darling!" she murmured, trembling with joy. "Vladimir Platonych, from where has God sent you?"

"I want to settle here for good," he told her. "I have resigned my position and have come here to try my fortune as a free man and lead a settled life. Besides, it's time to send my boy to school. He is grown up now. You know, my wife and I have become reconciled."

"Where is she?" asked Olenka.

"At the hotel with the boy. I am looking for lodgings."

"Good gracious, bless you, take my house. Why won't my house do? Oh, dear! Why, I won't ask any rent of you," Olenka burst out in the greatest excitement, and began to cry again. "You live here, and the wing will be enough for me. Oh, Heavens, what a joy!"

The very next day the roof was being painted and the walls whitewashed, and Olenka, arms akimbo, was going about the yard superintending. Her face brightened with her old smile. Her whole being revived and freshened, as though she had awakened from a long sleep. The veterinarian's wife and child arrived. She was a thin, plain woman, with a crabbed expression. The boy Sasha, small for his ten years of age, was a chubby child, with clear blue eyes and dimples in his cheeks. He made for the kitten the instant he entered the yard, and the place rang with his happy laughter.

"Is that your cat, auntie?" he asked Olenka. "When she has little kitties, please give me one. Mamma is awfully afraid of mice."

Olenka chatted with him, gave him tea, and there was a sudden warmth in her bosom and a soft gripping at her heart, as though the boy were her own son.

In the evening, when he sat in the dining-room studying his lessons, she looked at him tenderly and whispered to herself:

"My darling, my pretty. You are such a clever child, so good to look at."

"An island is a tract of land entirely surrounded by water," he recited.

"An island is a tract of land," she repeated—the first idea asseverated with conviction after so many years of silence and mental emptiness.

She now had her opinions, and at supper discussed with Sasha's parents how difficult the studies had become for the children at school, but how, after all, a classical education was better than a commercial course, because when you graduated from school then the road was open to you for any career at all. If you chose to, you could become a doctor, or, if you wanted to, you could become an engineer.

Sasha began to go to school. His mother left on a visit to her sister in Kharkov and never came back. The father was away every day inspecting cattle, and sometimes was gone three whole days at a time, so that Sasha, it seemed to Olenka, was utterly abandoned, was treated as if he were quite superfluous, and must be dying of hunger. So she transferred him into the wing along with herself and fixed up a little room for him there.

Every morning Olenka would come into his room and find him sound asleep with his hand tucked under his cheek, so quiet that he seemed not to be breathing. What a shame to have to wake him, she thought.

"Sashenka," she said sorrowingly, "get up, darling. It's time to go to school."

He got up, dressed, said his prayers, then sat down to drink tea. He drank three glasses of tea, ate two large biscuits and half a buttered roll. The sleep was not yet out of him, so he was a little cross.

"You don't know your fable as you should, Sashenka," said Olenka, looking at him as though he were departing on a long journey. "What a lot of trouble you are. You must try hard and learn, dear, and mind your teachers."

"Oh, let me alone, please," said Sasha.

Then he went down the street to school, a little fellow wearing a large cap and carrying a satchel on his back. Olenka followed him noiselessly.

"Sashenka," she called.

He looked round and she shoved a date or a caramel into his hand. When he reached the street of the school, he turned around and said, ashamed of being followed by a tall, stout woman:

"You had better go home, auntie. I can go the rest of the way myself."

She stopped and stared after him until he had disappeared into the school entrance.

Oh, how she loved him! Not one of her other ties had been so deep. Never before had she given herself so completely, so disinterestedly, so cheerfully as now that her maternal instincts were all aroused. For this boy, who was not hers, for the dimples in his cheeks and for his big cap, she would have given her life, given it with joy and with tears of rapture. Why? Ah, indeed, why?

When she had seen Sasha off to school, she returned home quietly, content, serene, overflowing with love. Her face, which had grown younger in the last half year, smiled and beamed. People who met her were pleased as they looked at her.

"How are you, Olga Semyonovna, darling? How are you getting on, darling?"

"The school course is very hard nowadays," she told at the market. "It's no joke. Yesterday the first class had a fable to learn by heart, a Latin translation, and a problem. How is a little fellow to do all that?"

And she spoke of the teacher and the lessons and the text-books, repeating exactly what Sasha said about them.

At three o'clock they had dinner. In the evening they prepared the lessons together, and Olenka wept with Sasha over the difficulties. When she put him to bed, she lingered a long time making the sign of the cross over him and muttering a prayer. And when she lay in bed, she dreamed of the far-away, misty future when Sasha would finish his studies and become a doctor or an engineer, have a large house of his own, with horses and a carriage, marry, and have children. She would fall asleep still thinking of the same things, and tears would roll down her cheeks from her closed eyes. And the black cat would lie at her side purring: "Mrr, mrr, mrr."

Suddenly there was a loud knocking at the gate. Olenka woke up breathless with fright, her heart beating violently. Half a minute later there was another knock.

"A telegram from Kharkov," she thought, her whole body in a tremble. "His mother wants Sasha to come to her in Kharkov. Oh, great God!"

She was in despair. Her head, her feet, her hands turned cold. There was no unhappier creature in the world, she felt. But another minute passed, she heard voices. It was the veterinarian coming home from the club.

"Thank God," she thought. The load gradually fell from her heart, she was at ease again. And she went back to bed, thinking of Sasha who lay fast asleep in the next room and sometimes cried out in his sleep:

"I'll give it to you! Get away! Quit your scrapping!"

THE LADY WITH THE DOG

(*Дама с Собачкой*, 1899)

The most deeply revealing of Chekhov's stories begins in Yalta, the southern resort town on the Black Sea, where Chekhov himself had been living for the relief of his tubercular symptoms. Chekhov claimed that in his fictional works he never wrote about himself directly, but there is much in the feeling of this story that coincides with Chekhov's experience of falling in love with the actor Olga Knipper. Most significantly there is Gurov's wonder at himself, in the midst of a long, unhappy marriage and after countless affairs, that he has finally, really, fallen in love: "She sat down in the third row, and when Gurov looked at her his heart contracted, and he understood clearly that for him there was in the whole world no creature so near, so precious, and so important to him; she, this little woman, in no way remarkable, lost in a provincial crowd, with a vulgar lorgnette in her hand, filled his whole life now, was his sorrow and his joy, the one happiness that he now desired for himself, and to the sounds of the inferior orchestra, of the wretched provincial violins, he thought how lovely she was. He thought and dreamed."

Chekhov and Knipper wed in 1901—to the surprise of their friends and families. They were childless.

I

IT WAS SAID that a new person had appeared on the sea-front: a lady with a little dog. Dmitri Dmitrich Gurov, who had by then been two weeks at Yalta, and so was fairly at home there, had begun to take an interest in new arrivals. Sitting in Verney's pavilion, he saw, walking on the sea-front, a fair-haired young lady of medium height, wearing a béret; a white Pomeranian dog was running behind her.

And afterwards he met her in the public gardens and in the square several times a day. She was walking alone, always wearing the same béret, and always with the same white dog; no one knew who she was, and everyone called her simply "the lady with the dog."

"If she is here alone without a husband or friends, it wouldn't be amiss to make her acquaintance," Gurov reflected.

He was under forty, but he had a daughter already twelve years old, and two sons at school. He had been married young, when he was a student in his second year, and by now his wife seemed half as old again as he. She was a tall, erect woman with dark eyebrows, staid and dignified, and, as she said of herself, intellectual. She read a great deal, used phonetic spelling, called her husband, not Dmitri, but Dimitri, and he secretly considered her unintelligent, narrow, inelegant, was afraid of her, and did not like to be at home. He had begun being unfaithful to her long ago—had been unfaithful to her often, and, probably on that account, almost always spoke ill of women, and when they were talked about in his presence, used to call them "the lower race."

It seemed to him that he had been so schooled by bitter experience that he might call them what he liked, and yet he could not get on for two days together without "the lower race." In the society of men he was bored and not himself, with them he was cold and uncommunicative; but when he was in the company of women he felt free, and knew what to say to them and how to behave; and he was at ease with them even when he was silent. In his appearance, in his character, in his whole nature, there was something attractive and elusive which allured women and disposed them in his favor; he knew that, and some force seemed to draw him, too, to them.

Experience often repeated, truly bitter experience, had taught him long ago that with decent people, especially Moscow people—always slow to move and irresolute—every intimacy, which at first so agreeably diversifies life and appears a light and charming adventure, inevitably grows into a regular problem of extreme intricacy, and in the long run the situation becomes unbearable. But at every fresh meeting with an interesting woman this experience seemed to slip out of his memory, and he was eager for life, and everything seemed simple and amusing.

One evening he was dining in the public garden, and the lady in the béret came up slowly to take the next table. Her expression, her gait, her dress, and the way she did her hair told him that she was a lady, that she was married, that she was in Yalta for the first time and alone, and that she was dull there. . . . The stories told of the immorality in such places as Yalta are to a great extent untrue; he despised them, and knew that such stories were for the most part made up by persons who would themselves have been glad to sin if they had been able; but when the lady sat down at the next table three paces from him, he remembered these tales of easy conquests, of trips to the mountains, and the tempting thought of a swift, fleeting love affair, a romance with an unknown woman, whose name he did not know, suddenly took possession of him.

He beckoned coaxingly to the Pomeranian, and when the dog came up to him he shook his finger at it. The Pomeranian growled; Gurov shook his finger at it again.

The lady looked at him and at once dropped her eyes.

"He doesn't bite," she said, and blushed.

"May I give him a bone?" he asked; and when she nodded he asked courteously, "Have you been long in Yalta?"

"Five days."

"And I have already dragged out two weeks here."

There was a brief silence.

"Time goes fast, and yet it is so dull here!" she said, not looking at him.

"That's only the fashion to say it is dull here. A provincial will live in Belyov or Zhidra and not be dull, and when he comes here it's 'Oh, the dullness! Oh, the dust!' One would think he came from Grenada."

She laughed. Then both continued eating in silence, like strangers; but after dinner they walked side by side; and there sprang up between them the light jesting conversation of people who are free and satisfied, to whom it does not matter where they go or what they talk about. They walked and talked of the strange light on the sea: the water was of a soft, warm lilac hue, and there was a golden streak from the moon upon it. They talked of how sultry it was after a hot day. Gurov told her that he came from Moscow, that he had taken his degree in Arts, but had a post in a bank; that he had trained as an opera-singer, but had given it up, that he owned two houses in Moscow. . . . And from her he learned that she had grown up in Petersburg, but had lived in

S—— since her marriage two years before, that she was staying another month in Yalta, and that her husband, who needed a holiday too, might perhaps come and fetch her. She was not sure whether her husband had a post in a Crown Department or under the Provincial Council—and was amused by her own ignorance. And Gurov learnt, too, that she was called Anna Sergeyevna.

Afterwards he thought about her in his room at the hotel—thought she would certainly meet him next day; it would be sure to happen. As he got into bed he thought how lately she had been a girl at school, doing lessons like his own daughter; he recalled the diffidence, the angularity, that was still manifest in her laugh and her manner of talking with a stranger. This must have been the first time in her life she had been alone in surroundings in which she was followed, looked at, and spoken to merely from a secret motive which she could hardly fail to guess. He recalled her slender, delicate neck, her lovely gray eyes.

"There's something pathetic about her, anyway," he thought, and fell asleep.

II

A week had passed since they had made acquaintance. It was a holiday. It was sultry indoors, while in the street the wind whirled the dust round and round, and blew people's hats off. It was a thirsty day, and Gurov often went into the pavilion, and pressed Anna Sergeyevna to have syrup and water or an ice. One did not know what to do with oneself.

In the evening when the wind had dropped a little, they went out on the pier to see the steamer come in. There were a great many people walking about the harbor; they had gathered to welcome someone, bringing bouquets. And two peculiarities of a well-dressed Yalta crowd were very conspicuous: the elderly ladies were dressed like young ones, and there were great numbers of generals.

Owing to the roughness of the sea, the steamer arrived late, after the sun had set, and it was a long time turning about before it reached the pier. Anna Sergeyevna looked through her lorgnette at the steamer and the passengers as though looking for acquaintances, and when she turned to Gurov her eyes were shining. She talked a great deal and asked disconnected questions, forgetting the next moment what she had asked; then she dropped her lorgnette in the crush.

The festive crowd began to disperse; it was too dark to see people's faces. The wind had completely dropped, but Gurov and Anna Sergeyevna still stood as though waiting to see someone else come from the steamer. Anna Sergeyevna was silent now, and sniffed the flowers without looking at Gurov.

"The weather is better this evening," he said. "Where shall we go now? Shall we drive somewhere?"

She made no answer.

Then he looked at her intently, and all at once put his arm round her and kissed her on the lips, and breathed in the moisture and the fragrance of the flowers; and he immediately looked round him, anxiously wondering whether anyone had seen them.

"Let us go to your hotel," he said softly. And both walked quickly.

The room was close and smelt of the scent she had bought at the Japanese shop. Gurov looked at her and thought: "What different people one meets in the world!" From the past he preserved memories of careless, good-natured women, who loved cheerfully and were grateful to him for the happiness he gave them, however brief it might be; and of women like his wife who loved without any genuine feeling, with superfluous phrases, affectedly, hysterically, with an expression that suggested that it was not love nor passion, but something more significant; and of two or three others, very beautiful, cold women, on whose faces he had caught a glimpse of a rapacious expression—an obstinate desire to snatch from life more than it could give, and these were capricious, unreflecting, domineering, unintelligent women not in their first youth, and when Gurov grew cold to them their beauty excited his hatred, and the lace on their linen seemed to him like scales.

But in this case there was still the diffidence, the angularity of inexperienced youth, an awkward feeling; and there was a sense of consternation as though someone had suddenly knocked at the door. The attitude of Anna Sergeyevna—"the lady with the dog"—to what had happened was somehow peculiar, very grave, as though it were her fall—so it seemed, and it was strange and inappropriate. Her face dropped and faded, and on both sides of it her long hair hung down mournfully; she mused in a dejected attitude like "the woman who was a sinner" in an old-fashioned picture.

"It's wrong," she said. "You will be the first to despise me now."

There was a watermelon on the table. Gurov cut himself a slice and began eating it unhurriedly. There followed at least half an hour of silence.

Anna Sergeyevna was touching; there was about her the purity of a good, simple woman who had seen little of life. The solitary candle burning on the table threw a faint light on her face, yet it was clear that she was very unhappy.

"How could I despise you?" asked Gurov. "You don't know what you are saying."

"God forgive me," she said, and her eyes filled with tears. "It's awful."

"You seem to feel you need to be forgiven."

"Forgiven? No. I am a bad, low woman; I despise myself and don't attempt to justify myself. It's not my husband but myself I have deceived. And not only just now; I have been deceiving myself for a long time. My husband may be a good, honest man, but he is a flunkey! I don't know what he does there, what his work is, but I know he is a flunkey! I was twenty when I was married to him. I have been tormented by curiosity; I wanted something better. 'There must be a different sort of life,' I said to myself. I wanted to live! To live, to live! . . . I was fired by curiosity . . . you don't understand it, but, I swear to God, I could not control myself; something happened to me: I could not be restrained. I told my husband I was ill, and came here. . . . And here I have been walking about as though I were dazed, like a mad creature; . . . and now I have become a vulgar, contemptible woman whom anyone may despise."

Gurov felt bored already, listening to her. He was irritated by the naïve tone, by this remorse, so unexpected and inopportune; but for the tears in her eyes, he might have thought she was jesting or playing a part.

"I don't understand," he said softly. "What is it you want?"

She hid her face on his breast and pressed close to him.

"Believe me, believe me, I beseech you . . ." she said. "I love a pure, honest life, and sin is loathsome to me. I don't know what I am doing. Simple people say: 'The Evil One has beguiled me.' And I may say of myself now that the Evil One has beguiled me."

"Hush, hush! . . ." he muttered.

He looked at her fixed, scared eyes, kissed her, talked softly and affectionately, and by degrees she was comforted, and her gaiety returned; they both began laughing.

Afterwards when they went out there was not a soul on the sea-front. The town with its cypresses had quite a deathlike air, but the sea still broke noisily on the shore; a single barge was rocking on the waves, and a lantern was blinking sleepily on it.

They found a cab and drove to Oreanda.

"I found out your surname in the hall just now: it was written on the board—Von Diderits," said Gurov. "Is your husband a German?"

"No; I believe his grandfather was a German, but he is an Orthodox Russian himself."

At Oreanda they sat on a seat not far from the church, looked down at the sea, and were silent. Yalta was hardly visible through the morning mist; white clouds stood motionless on the mountaintops. The leaves did not stir on the trees, grasshoppers chirruped, and the monotonous hollow sound of the sea rising up from below, spoke of the peace, of the eternal sleep awaiting us. So it must have sounded when there was no Yalta, no Oreanda here; so it sounds now, and it will sound as indifferently and monotonously when we are all no more. And in this constancy, in this complete indifference to the life and death of each of us, there lies hid, perhaps, a pledge of our eternal salvation, of the unceasing movement of life upon earth, of unceasing progress towards perfection. Sitting beside a young woman who in the dawn seemed so lovely, soothed, and spellbound in these magical surroundings—the sea, mountains, clouds, the open sky—Gurov thought how in reality everything is beautiful in this world when one reflects: everything except what we think or do ourselves when we forget our human dignity and the higher aims of our existence.

A man walked up to them—probably a guard—looked at them and walked away. And this detail seemed mysterious and beautiful, too. They saw a steamer come from Theodosia, with its lights out in the glow of dawn.

"There is dew on the grass," said Anna Sergeyevna, after a silence.

"Yes. It's time to go home."

They went back to the town.

Then they met every day at twelve o'clock on the sea-front, lunched and dined together, went for walks, admired the sea. She complained that she slept badly, that her heart throbbed violently; asked the same questions, troubled now by jealousy and now by the fear that he did not respect her sufficiently. And often in the square or gardens, when there was no one near them, he suddenly drew her to him and kissed her passionately. Complete idleness, these kisses in broad daylight while he looked round in dread of someone's seeing them, the heat, the smell of the sea, and the continual passing to and fro before him of idle, well-dressed, well-fed people, made a new man of him; he told Anna Sergeyevna how beautiful she was, how fascinating. He was impatiently passionate, he would not move a step away from her, while she was often pensive and continually urged him to confess that he did not respect her, did not love her in the least, and thought of her as nothing but a common woman. Rather late almost every evening they drove somewhere out of town, to Oreanda or to the waterfall; and the expedition was always a success, the scenery invariably impressed them as grand and beautiful.

They were expecting her husband to come, but a letter came from him, saying that there was something wrong with his eyes, and he entreated his wife to come home as quickly as possible. Anna Sergeyevna made haste to go.

"It's a good thing I am going away," she said to Gurov. "It's the finger of destiny!"

She went by coach and he went with her. They were driving the whole day. When she had got into a compartment of the express, and when the second bell had rung, she said:

"Let me look at you once more . . . look at you once again. That's right."

She did not shed tears, but was so sad that she seemed ill, and her face was quivering.

"I shall remember you . . . think of you," she said. "God be with you; be happy. Don't remember evil against me. We are parting forever—it must be so, for we ought never to have met. Well, God be with you."

The train moved off rapidly, its lights soon vanished from sight, and a minute later there was no sound of it, as though everything had conspired together to end as quickly as possible that sweet delirium, that madness. Left alone on the platform, and gazing into the dark distance, Gurov listened to the chirrup of the grasshoppers and the hum of the telegraph wires, feeling as though he had only just waked up. And he thought, musing, that there had been another episode or adventure in his life, and it, too, was at an end, and nothing was left of it but a memory. . . . He was moved, sad, and conscious of a slight remorse. This young woman whom he would never meet again had not been happy with him; he was genuinely warm and affectionate with her, but yet in his manner, his tone, and his caresses there had been a shade of light irony, the coarse condescension of a happy man who was, besides, almost twice her age. All the time she had called him kind, exceptional, lofty; obviously he had seemed to her different from what he really was, so he had unintentionally deceived her. . . .

Here at the station was already a scent of autumn; it was a cold evening.

"It's time for me to go north," thought Gurov as he left the platform. "High time!"

III

At home in Moscow everything was in its winter routine; the stoves were heated, and in the morning it was still dark when the children were having breakfast and getting ready for school, and the nurse would light the lamp for a short time. The frosts had begun already. When the first snow has fallen, on the first day of sledge-driving it is pleasant to see the white earth, the white roofs, to draw soft, delicious breath, and the season brings back the days of one's youth. The old limes and birches, white with hoar-frost, have a good-natured expression; they are nearer to one's heart than cypresses and palms, and near them one doesn't want to be thinking of the sea and the mountains.

Gurov was Moscow born; he arrived in Moscow on a fine frosty day, and when he put on his fur coat and warm gloves, and walked along Petrovka, and when on Saturday evening he heard the ringing of the bells, his recent trip and the places he had seen lost all charm for him. Little by little he became absorbed in Moscow life, greedily read three newspapers a day, and declared he did not read the Moscow papers on principle! He already felt a longing to go to restaurants, clubs, dinner-parties, anniversary celebrations, and he felt flattered at entertaining distinguished lawyers and artists, and at playing cards with a professor at the doctors' club. He could already eat a whole plateful of salt fish and cabbage.

In another month, he fancied, the image of Anna Sergeyevna would be shrouded in a mist in his memory, and only from time to time would visit him in his dreams with a touching smile as others did. But more than a month passed, real winter had come, and everything was still clear in his memory as though he had parted with Anna Sergeyevna only the day before. And his memories glowed more and more vividly. When in the evening stillness he heard from his study the voices of his children, preparing their lessons, or when he listened to a song or the organ at the restaurant, or the storm howled in the chimney, suddenly everything would rise up in his memory: what had happened on the pier, and the early morning with the mist on the mountains, and the steamer coming from Theodosia, and the kisses. He would pace a long time about his room, remembering it all and smiling; then his memories passed into dreams, and in his fancy the past was mingled with what was to come. Anna Sergeyevna did not visit him in dreams, but followed him about everywhere like a shadow and haunted him. When he shut his eyes he saw her as though she were living before him, and she seemed to him lovelier, younger, tenderer than she was; and he imagined himself finer than he had been in Yalta. In the evenings she peeped out at him from the bookcase, from the fireplace, from the corner—he heard her breathing, the caressing rustle of her dress. In the street he watched the women, looking for someone like her.

He was tormented by an intense desire to confide his memories to someone. But in his home it was impossible to talk of his love, and he had no one outside; he could not talk to his tenants nor to anyone at the bank. And what had he to talk of? Had he been in love, then? Had there been anything beautiful, poetical, or edifying or simply interesting in his relations with Anna Sergeyevna? And there was nothing for him but to talk vaguely of love, of woman, and no one guessed what it meant; only his wife twitched her black eyebrows, and said:

"The part of a lady-killer does not suit you at all, Dimitri."

One evening, coming out of the doctors' club with an official with whom he had been playing cards, he could not resist saying:

"If only you knew what a fascinating woman I made the acquaintance of in Yalta!"[1]

The official got into his sledge and was driving away, but turned suddenly and shouted:

"Dmitri Dmitrich!"

---

[1] In the original publication of the story, Gurov manages to add here: "*One couldn't say she was especially beautiful, but the impression she made on me was irresistible. Ever since I haven't been myself.*"

"What?"

"You were right this evening: the sturgeon was a bit too strong!"

These words, so ordinary, for some reason moved Gurov to indignation, and struck him as degrading and unclean. What savage manners, what people! What senseless nights, what uninteresting, uneventful days! The rage for card-playing, the gluttony, the drunkenness, the continual talk always about the same thing. Useless pursuits and conversations always about the same things absorb the better part of one's time, the better part of one's strength, and in the end there is left a life groveling and curtailed, worthless and trivial, and there is no escaping or getting away from it—just as though one were in a madhouse or a prison.

Gurov did not sleep all night, and was filled with indignation. And he had a headache all next day. And the next night he slept badly; he sat up in bed, thinking, or paced up and down his room. He was sick of his children, sick of the bank; he had no desire to go anywhere or to talk of anything.

In the holidays in December he prepared for a journey, and told his wife he was going to Petersburg to do something in the interests of a young friend—and he set off for S——. What for? He did not very well know himself. He wanted to see Anna Sergeyevna and to talk with her—to arrange a meeting, if possible.

He reached S—— in the morning, and took the best room at the hotel, in which the floor was covered with gray army cloth, and on the table was an inkstand, gray with dust and adorned with a figure on horseback, with its hat in its hand and its head broken off. The hotel porter gave him the necessary information; Von Diderits lived in a house of his own in Old Goncharnaya Street—it was not far from the hotel: he was rich and lived in good style, and had his own horses; everyone in the town knew him. The porter pronounced the name "Dridirits."

Gurov went without haste to Old Goncharnaya Street and found the house. Just opposite the house stretched a long, gray fence adorned with nails.

"One would run away from a fence like that," thought Gurov, looking from the fence to the windows of the house and back again.

He considered: today was a holiday, and the husband would probably be at home. And in any case it would be tactless to go into the house and upset her. If he were to send her a note it might fall into her husband's hands, and then it might ruin everything. The best thing was to trust to chance. And he kept walking up and down the street by the fence, waiting for the chance. He saw a beggar go in at the gate and dogs fly at him; then an hour later he heard a piano, and the sounds were faint and indistinct. Probably it was Anna Sergeyevna playing. The front door suddenly opened, and an old woman came out, followed by the familiar white Pomeranian. Gurov was on the point of calling to the dog, but his heart began beating violently, and in his excitement he could not remember the dog's name.

He walked up and down, and loathed the gray fence more and more, and by now he thought irritably that Anna Sergeyevna had forgotten him, and was perhaps already amusing herself with someone else, and that that was very natural in a young woman who had nothing to look at from morning till night but that confounded fence. He went back to his hotel room and sat for a long while on the sofa, not knowing what to do, then he had dinner and a long nap.

"How stupid and worrying it is!" he thought when he woke and looked at the dark windows: it was already evening. "Here I've had a good sleep for some reason. What shall I do in the night?"

He sat on the bed, which was covered by a cheap gray blanket, such as one sees in hospitals, and he taunted himself in his vexation:

"So much for the lady with the dog . . . so much for the adventure. . . . You're in a nice fix. . . ."

That morning at the station a poster in large letters had caught his eye. *The Geisha* was to be performed for the first time. He thought of this and went to the theater.

"It's quite possible she may go to the first performance," he thought.

The theater was full. As in all provincial theaters, there was a fog above the chandelier, the gallery was noisy and restless; in the front row the local dandies were standing up before the beginning of the performance, with their hands behind them; in the Governor's box the Governor's daughter, wearing a boa, was sitting in the front seat, while the Governor himself lurked modestly behind the curtain with only his hands visible; the orchestra was a long time tuning up; the stage curtain swayed. All the time the audience were coming in and taking their seats Gurov looked at them eagerly.

Anna Sergeyevna, too, came in. She sat down in the third row, and when Gurov looked at her his heart contracted, and he

understood clearly that for him there was in the whole world no
creature so dear, so precious, and so important to him; she, this
little woman, in no way remarkable, lost in a provincial crowd,
with a vulgar lorgnette in her hand, filled his whole life now, was
his sorrow and his joy, the one happiness that he now desired for
himself, and to the sounds of the inferior orchestra, of the wretched
provincial violins, he thought how lovely she was. He thought and
dreamed.

A young man with small side-whiskers, tall and stooping, came
in with Anna Sergeyevna and sat down beside her; he bent his head
at every step and seemed to be continually bowing. Most likely this
was the husband whom at Yalta, in a rush of bitter feeling, she had
called a flunkey. And there really was in his long figure, his side-
whiskers, and the small bald patch on his head, something of the
flunkey's obsequiousness; his smile was sugary, and in his buttonhole
there was some badge of distinction like the number on a waiter.

During the first interval the husband went away to smoke; she
remained alone in her stall. Gurov, who was sitting in the stalls, too,
went up to her and said in a trembling voice, with a forced smile:

"Good evening."

She glanced at him and turned pale, then glanced again with
horror, unable to believe her eyes, and tightly gripped the fan and
the lorgnette in her hands, evidently struggling with herself not to
faint. Both were silent. She was sitting; he was standing, frightened
by her confusion and not venturing to sit down beside her. The
violins and the flute began tuning up. He felt suddenly frightened;
it seemed as though all the people in the boxes were looking at
them. She got up and went quickly to the door; he followed her,
and both walked senselessly along passages, and up and down stairs,
and figures in legal, scholastic, and civil service uniforms, all
wearing badges, flitted before their eyes. They caught glimpses of
ladies, of fur coats hanging on pegs; the drafts blew on them,
bringing a smell of stale tobacco. And Gurov, whose heart was
beating violently, thought:

"Oh, heavens! Why are these people here and this orchestra! . . ."

And at that instant he recalled how when he had seen Anna
Sergeyevna off at the station he had thought that everything was
over and they would never meet again. But how far they were still
from the end!

On the narrow, gloomy staircase over which was written "To
the Amphitheater," she stopped.

"How you have frightened me!" she said, breathing hard, still pale and overwhelmed. "Oh, how you have frightened me! I am half dead. Why have you come? Why?"

"But do understand, Anna, do understand . . ." he said hastily in a low voice. "I entreat you to understand. . . ."

She looked at him with dread, with entreaty, with love; she looked at him intently, to keep his features more distinctly in her memory.

"I am so unhappy," she went on, not heeding him. "I have thought of nothing but you all the time; I live only in the thought of you. And I wanted to forget, to forget you; but why, oh, why, have you come?"

On the landing above them two schoolboys were smoking and looking down, but that was nothing to Gurov; he drew Anna Sergeyevna to him, and began kissing her face, her cheeks, and her hands.

"What are you doing, what are you doing!" she cried in horror, pushing him away. "We are mad. Go away today; go away at once. . . . I beseech you by all that is sacred, I implore you. . . . There are people coming this way!"

Someone was coming up the stairs.

"You must go away," Anna Sergeyevna went on in a whisper. "Do you hear, Dmitri Dmitrich? I will come and see you in Moscow. I have never been happy; I am miserable now, and I never, never shall be happy, never! Don't make me suffer still more! I swear I'll come to Moscow. But now let us part. My precious, good, dear one, we must part!"

She pressed his hand and began rapidly going downstairs, looking round at him, and from her eyes he could see that she really was unhappy. Gurov stood for a little while, listened, then, when all sound had died away, he found his coat and left the theater.

IV

And Anna Sergeyevna began coming to see him in Moscow. Once in two or three months she left S——, telling her husband that she was going to consult a doctor about an internal complaint—and her husband believed her, and did not believe her. In Moscow she stayed at the Slaviansky Bazaar hotel, and at once sent a man in a red cap to Gurov. Gurov went to see her, and no one in Moscow knew of it.

Once he was going to see her in this way on a winter morning (the messenger had come the evening before when he was out). With him walked his daughter, whom he wanted to take to school: it was on the way. Snow was falling in big, wet flakes.

"It's three degrees above freezing-point, and yet it is snowing," said Gurov to his daughter. "The thaw is only on the surface of the earth; there is quite a different temperature at a greater height in the atmosphere."

"And why are there no thunderstorms in the winter, father?"

He explained that, too. He talked, thinking all the while that he was going to see her, and no living soul knew of it, and probably never would know. He had two lives: one, open, seen and known by all who cared to know, full of relative truth and of relative falsehood, exactly like the lives of his friends and acquaintances; and another life running its course in secret. And through some strange, perhaps accidental, conjunction of circumstances, everything that was essential, of interest and of value to him, everything in which he was sincere and did not deceive himself, everything that made the kernel of his life, was hidden from other people; and all that was false in him, the sheath in which he hid himself to conceal the truth—such, for instance, as his work in the bank, his discussions at the club, his "lower race," his presence with his wife at anniversary festivities—all that was open. And he judged of others by himself, not believing in what he saw, and always believing that every man had his real, most interesting life under the cover of secrecy and under the cover of night. All personal life rested on secrecy, and possibly it was partly on that account that civilized man was so nervously anxious that personal privacy should be respected.

After leaving his daughter at school, Gurov went on to the Slaviansky Bazaar. He took off his fur coat below, went upstairs, and softly knocked at the door. Anna Sergeyevna, wearing his favorite gray dress, exhausted by the journey and the suspense, had been expecting him since the evening before. She was pale; she looked at him, and did not smile, and he had hardly come in when she fell on his breast. Their kiss was slow and prolonged, as though they had not met for two years.

"Well, how are you getting on there?" he asked. "What news?"

"Wait; I'll tell you directly. . . . I can't talk."

She could not speak; she was crying. She turned away from him, and pressed her handkerchief to her eyes.

"Let her have her cry out. I'll sit down and wait," he thought, and he sat down in an arm-chair.

Then he rang and asked for tea to be brought him, and while he drank his tea she remained standing at the window with her back to him. She was crying from emotion, from the miserable consciousness that their life was so hard for them; they could only meet in secret, hiding themselves from people, like thieves! Was not their life shattered?

"Come, do stop!" he said.

It was evident to him that this love of theirs would not soon be over, that he could not see the end of it. Anna Sergeyevna grew more and more attached to him. She adored him, and it was unthinkable to say to her that it was bound to have an end some day; besides, she would not have believed it!

He went up to her and took her by the shoulders to say something affectionate and cheering, and at that moment he saw himself in the looking-glass.

His hair was already beginning to turn gray. And it seemed strange to him that he had grown so much older, so much plainer during the last few years. The shoulders on which his hands rested were warm and quivering. He felt compassion for this life, still so warm and lovely, but probably already not far from beginning to fade and wither like his own. Why did she love him so much? He always seemed to women different from what he was, and they loved in him not himself, but the man created by their imagination, whom they had been eagerly seeking all their lives; and afterwards, when they noticed their mistake, they loved him all the same. And not one of them had been happy with him. Time passed, he had made their acquaintance, got on with them, parted, but he had never once loved; it was anything you like, but not love.

And only now when his head was gray he had fallen properly, really in love—for the first time in his life.

Anna Sergeyevna and he loved each other like people very close and akin, like husband and wife, like tender friends; it seemed to them that fate itself had meant them for one another, and they could not understand why he had a wife and she a husband; and it was as though they were a pair of birds of passage, caught and forced to live in different cages. They forgave each other for what they were ashamed of in their past, they forgave everything in the present, and felt that this love of theirs had changed them both.

In moments of depression in the past he had comforted himself with any arguments that came into his mind, but now he no longer cared for arguments; he felt profound compassion, he wanted to be sincere and tender. . . .

"Don't cry, my darling," he said. "You've had your cry; that's enough. . . . Let us talk now, let us think of some plan."

Then they spent a long while taking counsel together, talked of how to avoid the necessity for secrecy, for deception, for living in different towns and not seeing each other for long at a time. How could they be free from this intolerable bondage?

"How? How?" he asked, clutching his head. "How?"

And it seemed as though in a little while the solution would be found, and then a new and splendid life would begin; and it was clear to both of them that they had still a long, long road before them, and that the most complicated and difficult part of it was only just beginning.